FALLEN

ARIA GLAZKI

ANIKA PRESS

WHEN WE ARE AFRAID, WE PULL BACK FROM LIFE. WHEN WE ARE IN LOVE, WE OPEN TO ALL THAT LIFE HAS TO OFFER WITH PASSION, EXCITEMENT, AND ACCEPTANCE.

—JOHN LENNON

PART I

CHAPTER ONE

VIOLETTA DORÉE IS BREATHTAKING. No other word could do her justice. Along with my breath, she stole my heart the first time I saw her, almost a year ago now.

Ever since, I've tagged along to more of Grayson's outlandishly opulent outings. Sumptuous hedonism surrounds us as I witness the affluent few indulge their every whim.

I came to New York to steep myself in its architecture, to lose myself in the lines and flourishes and history, to learn as much from the influence of past greats as from my higher-ups at Lynch & Co.

But once I saw Violetta, no splendor of the city could draw me away.

She is flawless, from the cascade of her dark-blonde hair, to the tantalizing swell of her breasts; from the endless lengths of her legs, to the intrigue of her upturned mouth and the spark in her piercingly blue eyes. Eyes that promise untold delights but can't hide an astute resolve.

The darling of the elite, Violetta is the shining center to their gaiety, invited to every event she doesn't host herself.

"She lives for a good party," Grayson informed me once, catching me staring.

She, too, was born outside this world of flowing spirits and ceaseless merriment. But unlike me she has penetrated it brilliantly, perhaps effortlessly, with her combination of beauty, charisma, and enthusiasm. Now, she is adored.

And the moment I saw her, laughing by a glittering champagne tower, she became loved.

Frequent peals of laughter break through the thrum of chatter filling William's penthouse. I trade my empty glass for a fresh one, luxuriating in the unabashed revelry. Deft waiters circulate expertly prepared delicacies and superb wines. Every face sports a delighted smile. And why shouldn't they?

This is my reintroduction into the world, and I have been missed.

Even Doctor Greenfield decided to attend, though he stands off to the side, unused to our boundless mirth. This room has no care for the trivialities of everyday life that weigh down his days. As I watch, Finley—my only competition for the title of premier hostess—aptly draws the doctor into conversation, saving me the trip across the room.

Instead, I exchange a flurry of kisses and greetings with well-wishing latecomers. Seconds after I turn away, Grayson's friendly face appears before me. His familiar hand presses mine. "How are you, Vi?"

"Better now," I assure, using my champagne to gesture around us. "What do you think?"

"You've been good for him." Grayson's gaze takes in the room before returning to me. "Braxton has finally learned to throw a decent party. Guess you can teach an old dog new tricks, though we're all looking forward to your next masterpiece."

"Soon enough," I promise with my best mysterious smile, ignoring his unsubtle dig at William. This is a perfectly respectable cocktail party, considering he had to plan it without my help. Lacking in creativity, maybe, but William is a businessman, not a socialite.

Grayson steers me to an empty spot on a nearby couch and perches on the armrest, bending toward me. "You look stunning, of course."

"Of course," I echo. A day of pampering at the spa guaranteed I look my best for tonight. A waiter offering crab beignets briefly interrupts us, and we both indulge. I snag the opportunity to verify the other servers are well spaced throughout William's expansive living room.

"So..." Grayson says when the waiter moves on.

"So?" I murmur, lifting my glass to acknowledge Karolina's wave.

"Bored with me already?"

Grayson is many things, but never boring. Charmingly oblivious, though. And there's no reason to stroke his ego, so I shrug, crooking an eyebrow.

"How can I redeem myself?" he teases.

I slide my gaze over him, down and up, just slowly enough for his smirk to slip. "Tell me something I haven't heard."

He recovers quickly, flashing me that trademark, cheeky smile—the one that says he doesn't have a care in the world and makes you believe, however briefly, that you shouldn't, either. "That's easy."

"Not for most." Even if I have been out of commission awhile.

Grayson stalls, swirling the golden liquor in his hand. "No," he muses, "maybe I shouldn't say."

"Well if it's not worth sharing…"

Unlike most of our friends, Grayson can keep a secret. But we both know he won't resist telling me now that he's caught my attention.

He leans closer, a devilish gleam in his eyes. "My friend Adrian has quite the crush on you."

That is news, but I shrug again, lightly shifting the fall of my hair on my shoulders. Grayson's shadow has lurked around, but I couldn't have pointed him out from the fluid collection of plus ones. Let him enjoy the pleasures we can offer, if Grayson wants him here. "You introduced him to our world, yet blame me for his infatuation with it?"

"You are blameless as ever, Vi. But he believes himself in love," Grayson says, lilting the final word like a schoolboy.

"Poor fool. Love doesn't last." This room is littered with lovers of my past. I lean back into the couch, welcoming the soft comfort. "Only pleasure counts."

Laughing, Grayson raises his glass.

I tap mine against it then lift the resonating crystal flute to my mouth.

Grayson's eyes catch the gentle parting of my lips, watching the trickle of champagne. Even he once wanted me. But choosing William allowed me more freedom, and Grayson's desire, like so many others', has morphed into an easy fondness. It helps that no one dares risk exclusion from my parties.

It also helps that I am dying.

But as I die, Manhattan's elite embraces me, wrapping me in all the pleasures endless wealth can offer in its attempt to stave off the inevitable.

CHAPTER TWO

"SHE SHOULDN'T BE HERE." With the party at Braxton's last night and now today's benefit, diving back into the rush of her social life can't be easy on her.

"What are you on about?" Grayson asks, handing me a scotch he knows I won't drink. A second later, his eyes find Violetta, posing for a photographer in front of the Revson Fountain. "Oh, of course. Do you ever think about anything else?"

"Frequently." I back the lie up by turning toward him, leaving Violetta in my periphery. She laughs, her shoulders lifting for a moment before her head tips back.

"This is getting old," Grayson comments, not for the first time. "Look around. Don't you think it's time to move on?"

Sunshine floods the plaza, glinting off sequins and jewelry and airborne droplets from the fountain. Swells of laughter and conversation surround us, punctuated by the clink of glasses marking private toasts. Discreet bar and appetizer stations edge the clusters of guests. Grayson drains his tumbler then trades it for my full one.

"Love doesn't work like that," I finally say.

He snorts, almost choking on his drink. His free hand lands on my shoulder. "Love isn't real. And everybody"—he underscores the word by swinging his other hand around the crowd—"here knows it. Except for you." He smiles, shaking his head as he often has at my faith in the face of his jadedness.

A family friend or business contact approaches, and Grayson relents, sliding into the casual formality of the fundraiser. Unimportant, unnoticed, and relieved, I step away, discarding the empty tumbler on a passing waiter's tray. Since our days at Cornell, Grayson has tugged me into this world of exclusive events, grooming me, teaching me to navigate the social minefield on stray weekend visits to the city. Some once believed we were lovers; more still hardly noticed my existence. A few I have pursued in my bumbling attempts to network.

Only one have I never approached despite the aching desire to know her.

William Braxton stands at her side as they both engage the flurry of people around them. Her smile fades for a moment into fatigue, but of course he doesn't notice.

Chiming sounds as ushers make the rounds ringing delicate bells, and the murmurs change as guests trickle into the open doors of the David H. Koch Theater. Braxton offers Violetta his arm, leading her inside. Will I be able to see her from my seat? I'm in no rush to be disappointed.

One flight up, I see the two of them again.

"I'll be in in a minute." Her voice is unmistakable, even amid the chatter of guests heading to their seats.

Braxton's grim expression halts my progress up the stairs. I pull out my phone, stepping toward the window as an excuse to linger, as if what matters are the concentric circles of the emptying Robertson Plaza below.

"Really, it's fine," Violetta assures, shooing him away.

At his departure, her eyes drift shut, and her smile disappears. A heartbeat later she turns and strides away from the entrance to the first ring, then sinks onto a plush bench. A man I don't recognize steps toward her, but she sends him off with a wan smile, a poor double for her usual brilliance.

Soon only we remain. She pulls a tissue from her purse and brings it to her mouth, burying the cough that shakes her. Pink crests her cheeks from the effort.

"Are you all right?" I ask idiotically, coming toward her.

Her gaze lands on me, and I forget everything else.

"I'm fine," she lies, dismissing me like the others.

But I can't just walk away. "Can I bring you something? Some water?"

"You'll miss the ballet." She pastes on another smile. "I'll be all right."

"I don't mind waiting, if you'd like."

Her eyes narrow, seeing through me. "You know," she states.

Everyone knows, but I settle for a simple, "Yes."

Tension seeps from her, gently crumpling her posture as her head tilts back. Her lips part to welcome in the air. The faint sound of the overture underscores the rasp of her breath. "Do I know you?" she asks, unusually solemn.

"Adrian Thompson."

A light chuckle replaces her exhale as the corners of her lips edge up. "Grayson's friend?"

So this is Adrian, the friend Grayson adopted into this life out of idle curiosity then grew to like, and now the poor boy's head over heels for the decadence of Manhattan's social scene.

Of course, I can't blame him. I ran here at eighteen and never look back, embracing every pleasure I can find.

"Are you feeling better?" He doesn't move closer, as though he's scared to be near me.

I swipe under my lips with a tissue, catching any stray lipstick. "It doesn't get better than me," I tease, standing. William will be wondering where I am. He doesn't even like the ballet.

"No," Adrian says, smiling just enough to reveal a hint of a dimple. "It certainly doesn't."

There's something so impossibly earnest about him. It's almost charming, his naiveté. "That's quite the line."

His eyes don't leave me. I fluff my hair and shrug my shoulders, posing for effect, but he doesn't smile now. "Stunning," he calls me, still serious.

My chuckle transforms into another cough, pulling him closer. His hand hovers above my arm until I step away. "You're sweet. You should go, have a good time. That's why we're here, after all."

His hands find his pockets. "And here I thought we were here to raise money for the ballet."

"They're here to raise money. We're here to enjoy it," I add, spinning away to enter the theater.

CHAPTER THREE

"*WHO IS THAT*?" Finley's question instantly disperses the tittering group around me.

A tray of mimosas floats past us, but I reach instead for a hand-painted truffle. "Who?" The chocolate melts smoothly in my mouth.

"Over there." She nods toward a corner by the floor-to-ceiling windows.

Light streams onto a secluded settee with a lone figure sitting, staring outside. I turn my back.

"Have I seen him before?" Finley's head tilts as she takes in Adrian's box-store khakis and sweater. "Prudence will really invite anyone, won't she."

"He's Grayson's pet project," I explain.

"Well, he is kind of cute. Sort of like a puppy." A mischievous smile later, she strides off.

Good. Maybe she'll redirect his little crush.

"Are you enjoying yourself?" William asks, stretching out a fresh Bellini for me.

"Aren't you?" I should probably find something substantial to eat before drinking anything more. Finally a tray of chèvre-and-honey toast points is in sight.

William trails me around a cream sitting area. "I was hoping to spend some time alone with you."

"No strenuous activity allowed," I remind. It hasn't been all that long since I left the hospital.

William's eyes focus on the breadcrumb I lick from my bottom lip. "Nothing strenuous." The ice in his tumbler clinks as he drinks. "How about I take you home?"

"I'm not ready to go yet." I turn away to nab another passing hors d'oeuvre.

His hand finds my lower back, thumb brushing skin exposed by a deep vee. "We could relax. I could give you a massage… And, impossible as you are, I have a surprise for you."

"A surprise?" Glancing over my shoulder brings me intimately close, so I can smell the whiskey on his breath, see every glint of silver streaking through his hair. William's surprises usually involve diamonds. "I guess Prue wouldn't mind if we left early."

His smiling lips chastely brush mine. "I'll call for the car."

When Braxton leaves her, Violetta scans the room, seeking something in a rare moment of peace. She sips her drink then stumbles, and I'm by her side before my brain catches up. I let go almost as soon as I touch her, but my palm burns from the contact. I bury my hands in my pockets so I won't reach for her again.

"Are you all right?" My heart flutters at our proximity.

"Grayson's friend," she murmurs, her full lips curving slightly. "Are you always this concerned?"

"About you," I hear my own lips say.

She chuckles, absently bringing her glass to her mouth then letting it drift down again without sipping. "You don't even know me. I am not some token wonder for you to adore."

"And I am not so easily enticed." Though I should have known Grayson wouldn't keep his mouth shut forever. And now that she knows, what must she think of me? At least she hasn't walked away.

"I don't much care for all this…indulgence," I confess to keep our brief encounter going a moment longer. In my time on the periphery, I have witnessed far too much of the scandals and false friendships to have much of a taste for any of it. Except for her.

"And yet, here you are."

"I wouldn't be, if you would agree to see me elsewhere." The lush atmosphere, or an earlier mimosa, or the delicate scent of her perfume have made me overly bold, but the light purse to her lips and a crook in her eyebrow prevent me from taking it back. I may never have another chance to speak to her like this.

"Why would I stoke your infatuation? Look around," she adds before my jumbled mind can respond. "Half the men here would profess their devotion to me, given the chance, each one offering more than you ever could."

"And yet," I echo, intoxicated by her attention, "none of them can offer you what I can."

She laughs, but her headshake ends with her eyes gently narrowed on me. Braxton appears soundlessly at her side and bends to her ear, but still she watches me until he turns her toward the door. Her free hand snakes through her hair, shifting it over the nude expanse of her back. Braxton's arm curls over her hip as they leave.

"You know," a fresh voice purrs beside me, "Vi isn't the only girl here worth attention." Clara drops her weight into one hip and tilts her chin up.

"Don't bother." Grayson's impeccable timing saves me from correcting her. His arm lands around my shoulders. "He's smitten. And anyway." He lets me go, angling his body between Clara's and mine. "Why would you waste your time on him?"

Clara giggles, hunching her shoulders to showcase her chest. Perpetual playboy that he is, Grayson is still a greater "catch" than I could ever be, and his intercession serves me well on the rare occasion I catch someone's eye, allowing me to fade back into the background where I belong.

Hours later, buzzing on my wooden dining table offers a welcome distraction from the bank design I'm drafting, for practice more than anything. My boss probably won't even glance at it, but it's all part of paying my dues.

"Looks like you made quite the impression today," Grayson says the moment I answer the phone.

"Did I? And don't you have company?" Clara was fawning all over him when we left brunch, which would usually mean the rest of his day would be spent "entertaining."

"She's in the shower," he says offhand. "Aren't you the least bit curious who asked about you?"

"I didn't discuss business with anyone today, and you know I'm not interested in anything else." I stretch back in the chair to ease the stiffness in my shoulders, then lean forward and switch on a light to fight the growing darkness outside. Maybe I should make a fresh pot of coffee.

"That's a shame," Grayson says. "Vi will be disappointed. Until she finds her next little distraction, anyway."

"Wait." I let the papers I'm holding drop to the table and press my phone closer to my ear. "Wait, who?" He can't possibly have said what my exhausted brain just heard.

"Don't tell me you've forgotten the love of your life," he says drily.

"She said something about me?" I sound like a teenager, but my heart pounds on. Who needs coffee when the mere mention of Violetta sends adrenaline coursing through me?

"She said she wouldn't entirely mind if I gave you her number, if you weren't a complete psycho, that is."

I can picture him, lounging on his leather couch with a snifter of scotch, laughing at my fluster, my inexperience, the depth of my feelings. But the important part is that she spoke about me. She remembered me, enough to talk to Grayson. Enough to want me to call her. I scramble for my pen, digging it out from beneath the pile of sketches. "What is it?"

"Oh, have we decided you aren't a psycho?"

"Grayson!" This isn't something to joke about.

"Calm down." He rattles off the number. "But don't call her tonight," he adds quickly.

"I wasn't going to." What could I even say to her? My uncharacteristic boldness from this afternoon has long since dissipated. Calling Violetta would require a plan.

❧ Chapter Four ❧

MY PHONE CHIMING ACCOMPANIES my final pill's journey down my throat. Finley's face pops up on the screen, but I ignore it in favor of washing mine. We have plans to meet for Zumba, but I should go even if she wants to ditch me for something more *du jour*. And before I do, I should find something worthy of eating for breakfast, despite the nausea clinging to my esophagus.

William's latest gift winks at me under the lights of my vanity as I finish my makeup. My fingers trace the diamond bracelet on its velvet holder before I head to my closet. He really does have exquisite taste in jewelry. I should encourage him to expand that discrimination to food, maybe tonight for dinner, at Eleven Madison or Daniel.

Then again, he simply put me in the car last night, instead of driving me over to my apartment like he used to, so maybe I should make him wait a few days.

In the kitchen, my phone chimes again, and I swipe my thumb across the screen while staring into my fridge. "Let me guess, you want to cancel again."

Silence meets my statement.

"It's all right, Finley. I suppose I could be persuaded to forgive you." She doesn't need the cardio nearly as much as I do.

"I—I'm sorry," a male voice stutters.

I pull the phone from my ear, but the screen doesn't have a photo or name to jog my memory. I let the fridge door drift shut. "Who is this?"

"Adrian. Adrian Thompson? Grayson, he told me you would, well…"

My lips curve at the memory of his childish proclamations at Prue's party last weekend. "Well?"

"That you wouldn't be entirely opposed to my calling."

I can practically hear him hold his breath. He really is like an eager puppy.

"Depends on what you called to say."

"How are you?"

"That's it? Pretty unimaginative." Twenty minutes left before that class, but whatever scraps of motivation I had dredged up are now gone. Maybe I could catch the afternoon session instead.

"It's a start," Grayson's friend says with a touch more confidence.

"Skip ahead." Silence again. I lean against my fridge, waiting for him to muster up the shred of courage he showed at Prue's.

But it doesn't take long for him to ask, "What are you doing today?"

I must be dreaming, but if so, I'm happy to sleep forever. I've never been to Violetta's building before, but thanks to my years at Grayson's side, the doorman's scrutiny doesn't bother me. It isn't him I've come to impress.

The elevator ride stretches on and ends too soon. I swallow as much as my dry mouth allows, then exhale into my cupped hand before knocking on the door. Her door.

What am I doing?

The door opens, and the tilt of her head asks the same question. An eyebrow arches as her gaze falls to the meager bouquet in my hands. I hold out the camellias without a word—her favorite, always included in the arrangements at her parties.

Crinkling plastic underscores her laugh as she takes the bouquet and steps back, allowing me inside. The flowers land on a little lacquered table. Sunlight brightens her great room, which is bigger than my apartment, even if it is smaller than I would have thought.

"You can sit, you know," she offers, gesturing to plush furniture.

I clear the tickle from my throat to buy a second of time. She's wearing simple jeans today, with her hair pulled back. Blue eyes laugh at my hesitation.

"I thought we might go out," I finally say.

"And where would you take me?"

I decided this before I even called. "Perhaps to Brooklyn, to the beach." Low-key but still a treat. Plus the salt air would be good for her.

Derision marks the line of her eyebrows, but she can't hide her smile as she turns away and steps toward the windows. "You're so far out of your element in our world."

I shrug, taking the opportunity to loosen my shoulders. "You're no more of that world than I am."

A sharp spin turns her back to me with a scoff. "I may not have been born into money, but I was born to this lifestyle."

"What lifestyle is that, then?"

Customary flippancy replaces the momentary affront. "You, I suppose, would call it hedonism." Her tongue flicks over her bottom lip, and I know it's deliberate but cannot tear my eyes away. "Pleasure," she adds a moment later. "Nothing else matters. Not to me, and not to them."

I swallow the thickness in my throat. "Nothing?"

"That's the secret." She sinks onto an armchair, one of a pair demarcating the living and dining sections of the room. "There's nothing else to life."

My feet carry me closer. "Except love."

"Love?" she scoffs. "You really are adorable."

My silence stretches between us until she speaks again.

"Love is a fairytale. Live it if you like, but do it with someone else."

His gaze drops to the floor, discouraged perhaps. But better this idealism ends now than to let his delusion drag on. Maybe I shouldn't have indulged my curiosity at his expense.

He isn't so bad, though. Handsome even, despite his bargain sweater and fraying khakis. Dark features and a solid frame mark him with potential. "I could introduce you to anyone you want," I offer, inspired. It would be easy, really, to redirect his attention to someone more suited to his claims of love. Della, maybe?

His eyes catch mine again. "There is no one else."

"Do you hear yourself?" I was amused before, but his persistence is more annoying than flattering. "I know what I want out of life, and you aren't it." The pleasures of wealth could never be matched by foolish promises or fleeting passion.

My words are cruel—not what I intended when I agreed to his coming by—but he barely reacts. "Pleasure, then," he relents.

I relax into the cushions, exhaling. "See how quickly you forget your talk of love."

A small smile twists the corner of his lips. "How does the beach sound? You never answered."

Better than Zumba, at least. "I'll call for a car."

❧ CHAPTER FIVE ❧

"SO WHAT IS IT YOU DO, that allows you to take the day off like this?" A *pirozhok* warms my palms as Adrian and I stroll along Brighton Beach. The saltwater prickles inside my nose, down my throat. He doesn't know me but acts like he does, and my curiosity has warmed to him.

No one in my world does this—taking a spontaneous day off to hang out at the beach. In Brooklyn. Either they don't work, like me, leading a society lifestyle of leisure and decadence, or they do, in high-powered positions that don't allow for unplanned absences.

Adrian falls into neither category. Is he a transit worker? A waiter? Broad shoulders could mean his work is more physical. Construction? He's been entertaining so far, though. Intelligent, though I suppose he could have learned to fake it in a faulty attempt to blend in. How long ago did Grayson start letting him tag along?

"I'm an architect."

"An architect?" Who'd have thought. "Don't tell me, you design those tacky wedding chapels."

His smile rounds his cheeks, eliciting an uneven pair of dimples, deeper on his right side. "You caught me."

He's mellowed already, no longer skittish in talking to me. That glow of adulation has faded, too, replaced by something more quiet. Maybe reality doesn't match his earlier idolatry.

I pause, really looking at him for a moment. An architect could become something, if he wanted to work for it. "You should dress better," I point out.

Confusion flashes across his face at the change in topic, but he doesn't take his eyes off me.

"You could really make something of yourself, with the right projects, right clients," I explain. Thanks to Grayson, all the necessary connections wait at Adrian's fingertips. "And the right ones want to think you already have. Unfulfilled potential is risky, and they have too many established options."

"I never thought that much about it, I guess."

I turn away from his increasingly familiar hint of a smile and continue down the beach. "Dress for the job you want, for the *life* you want."

He falls into step beside me, hands tucked in his pockets. All day, he hasn't even tried to touch me, not taking any of the liberties a man used to power would.

"All I want is you."

A blue more captivating than the ocean stares at me, and I forget to breathe.

"You have to stop," Violetta says, frowning.

I never want to make her frown again. "You're right," I say, and she exhales with a slight shake of her head. "And if today is all about pleasure, what would you like to do next?"

Humor or mischief lights her eyes as she glances up at me.

"What's a visit to Little Odessa without a taste of the local delicacies?"

By the time we reach Glubina's door, Violetta's cheeks are flushed, and her breath comes more harshly despite our leisurely pace. But she doesn't let on, so I don't mention it.

"Inside or out?" The waiter's faint accent seems to underscore his utter disinterest in our business, but after two years in New York City, I'm used to being snubbed.

Violetta's easy self-assurance doesn't falter as she looks to me.

"Outside, maybe?" I ask. "It's such a beautiful day." And an illicit haze of smoke hangs inside, which her lungs could do without.

The waiter walks us a few steps away, gesturing to a glass-topped table. I hold a chair out for Violetta. As she steps close, a hint of her floral perfume reaches me, and I linger before stepping around to my own chair. Practiced twists of the waiter's hands hold menus out to us.

"We'll start with two flights of your vodkas," Violetta says without opening the faux-leather folder.

The waiter finally smiles as my mind stutters. Vodka in the middle of the day? "And some waters, please," I manage to add before he walks away.

Less than an hour later, miniature meat dumplings, a flaky pastry filled with oozing cheese, a potato-based salad, and more dishes Violetta ordered without hesitation stand partially consumed on the table.

All my years with Grayson, he's never once managed to convince me to try the supposed delicacy that salted fish eggs are. But one afternoon with Violetta and I'm converted, though it might be her blatant enjoyment of the nearly see-through pancakes and reddish globs that really does it.

"Eating well is one of life's greatest pleasures." She leans back with a smile, and I don't even think of disagreeing. Watching her eat certainly is.

"Do you truly enjoy it?" I ask without thinking. Shots of vodka flowing through my system have loosened my tongue, even if I drank them mostly to appease the glimpse of challenge in her eyes.

"The food?" Confused humor quirks her brow. Blonde wisps have escaped her ponytail, now framing her face. It is the most disheveled and relaxed I've ever seen her.

"Your life, the parties, playing hostess."

"Well I only 'play hostess,' as you call it, because my parties are the best. If you want something done right…" She lifts a shot glass, angling it in my direction before throwing her head back. "And when I host," she continues, "I get the best food, the best music, the best everything. Anything I'm in the mood for. Besides it's fun, being surrounded by people enjoying themselves. Hasn't Grayson brought you to my parties?"

"He has." Grayson wouldn't miss them, and of course given the choice, neither would I. It's no surprise she never noticed me.

She leans forward, bracing lightly against the table. "And you didn't enjoy them?"

How can I possibly explain the pleasure I feel from her proximity? And how those evenings spent watching her across the room pale in comparison, now, to being with her, talking to her, having daringly brushed my hand against hers once or twice.

"More than you know," I settle for saying.

She laughs, tilting her face up to the sunshine before looking out over the beach. The humor drops into something more serious as she watches the people or the waves, and then her lips part, her tongue sneaking out to moisten them.

"He doesn't love you, you know." The phrase escapes me, and I swallow roughly, damning the vodka.

Her gaze shifts back to me, but she pauses before answering quietly, "And I don't love him."

For a moment, the world stills. I thought I knew that, but hearing her say it changes everything. And nothing. I don't know what to say.

I shouldn't have said even what I have.

"You still don't understand, do you. Life, my life, it's about gratification, fulfillment. Satisfaction. And William, well." She pauses with a half-smile, lifting her previously untouched glass of water, lips twitching when she catches me watching her sip. "He's great in bed."

The poor boy looks like he's going to have a stroke. It shouldn't be funny, maybe, his untouched naiveté, but in a world of indulgent decadence, he's a peculiar rarity. From the color of his cheeks, you'd think he's never slept with anyone, much less enjoyed it.

He swallows roughly then asks, "And there's nothing else you like to do?" His eyes grow wide as his brain catches up. "Besides throwing the parties," he adds hastily.

"And going to the theater, and visiting Paris or Prague or Buenos Aires, and a well-timed joke, or a particularly fantastic massage…"

He's recovered quickly, his expression back to one of intent attention.

Dark eyes watch me as I inhale the salty air then add, "I enjoy everything I can."

❧ Chapter Six ❧

Days after our little beach trip, I don't know why I'm surprised to see Adrian and Dr. Greenfield tucked away in a corner, staring out the window as if the skyline is infinitely more interesting than anything within these walls. Of course the two outcasts would gravitate toward each other. But it's still unsettling, somehow.

"Well done, Vi." Grayson steps into my line of sight, holding out a fresh glass of champagne.

"You approve, do you?"

"I bow at the feet of the master." He actually does bow with an outdated flourish of his hand, smiling cheekily.

The small party isn't one of my best, certainly not a masterpiece, but it doesn't take much for my friends to enjoy themselves. That's the beauty, really—we're all inclined toward a good time. Add good drinks and sprinkle some sumptuousness into the menu, and we're guaranteed warm chatter and swells of laughter. It's mostly the guest list that makes a small affair like this successful.

So I guess I should be glad that Grayson brought Adrian along again, rather than leaving poor Dr. Greenfield without suitable company. There's just something about how comfortable the two of them seem together.

"Vi?" The syllable snaps me out of my thoughts. Grayson's pale-green eyes train sharply on me. "You all right?"

"Oh, I'm always all right." I add a smile, and after the briefest hesitation, his expression shifts back to nonchalance. "What were you saying?"

"Clara told me a delicious bit of gossip the other day."

"And what debauchery preceded her comments?"

Grayson fakes affront with a slight step back. "A gentleman never tells."

"Good thing you're a cad."

He grins, his eyebrows lifting briefly. To anyone who doesn't know better, his easy smile and light features would paint him as the picture of innocence. But those in this room know better.

Finley joins us, catching his expression. "What naughtiness are you two up to?"

"Oh, just discussing your latest fling with a certain bellhop," Grayson teases.

"A bellhop! As if." Finley turns a bit more toward me, physically blocking him from the conversation. "Vi, really, why do you insist on inviting such riffraff."

Grayson plucks a lobster flatbread from a waiter's tray, all too satisfied with himself. "There's no shame in slumming once in a while." Before Finley can respond, he adds, "Discretion, though. That's something you might want to look into."

Their bickering has once again given me a clear view of the doctor and Adrian. What could they possibly have to talk about so intently?

"Really, Vi, aren't you going to defend me?" Finley asks, her face flushed even through her makeup. Grayson must really have gotten to her.

"It's the twenty-first century," I point out. "Finley can sleep with whoever she wants."

Grayson's lips twitch, and he coughs to stifle a laugh.

"Vi! You know I'm seeing the Spanish ambassador. How could you believe I'd mess around with a bellboy?"

Oh, right. She had mentioned something, probably anyway. "Sorry, Finley." Not that she wouldn't in fact sleep with a yummy bellboy while trying to catch a more suitable suitor's eye, and hand.

I shake my head, trying to refocus on the party. I'm usually not this bad a hostess. A glance passes between my friends.

"Are you feeling all right?" Finley asks, echoing Grayson. The only thing these two don't fight about is me.

"I'm fine, really. Just worried about those two loners. They look much too serious."

My friends glance at the corner, where Adrian and the doctor are talking away, gesturing outside. Of course, William's view is considered one of the best in Manhattan.

"Well what do you expect when you invite the working class?" Finley asks.

"Even you're not that big a snob, Finley," I say.

Grayson snorts, but I have no intention of rising to the bait.

"What do you care? Let them talk, and keep out of the way." Finley twists an expertly dyed auburn lock then tosses it over her shoulder.

"They're my guests, I have to make sure they're enjoying themselves." The explanation sounds more like an excuse, to me anyway.

"Don't worry, Vi. Adrian and Greenfield get along perfectly well," Grayson says offhand, glancing around. His empty tumbler lands on a floating tray, and the server moves silently away to bring a refill.

"They know each other?" I ask.

Grayson freezes, and Finley perks up. We've clearly stumbled across a secret, and there's nothing she loves more than gossip—as long as it's not about her.

"You're so serious today, Vi." Grayson flashes me his trademark smile. "Is Braxton not doing his part to make you happy?"

"How do they know each other, Grayson?" I'm not in the mood for his flirtatious tricks.

He sighs, dropping the act. "They met at the hospital."

"The hospital?" Finley echoes as if the word is foreign.

"The lovesick fool visited every day you were there," Grayson admits with a small frown.

"We hadn't even met." My gaze flicks over to Adrian, but something's off. "I never saw him at the hospital." And I'd spent nearly a month there this time.

"He's not entirely an idiot," Grayson defends. "He knew he couldn't just walk into your room. But he went just about every day, asking about you. Apparently Greenfield took pity on him, shared what he could about your condition, let him put flowers outside your room."

My mind races back. I hadn't thought about it then, and I definitely haven't cared to since, but little bouquets of fresh flowers had been outside my room's interior window the entire time, set on a little table out of the nurses' way. Camellias, always. My favorites. Why would Adrian do that?

Grayson's hand lands lightly on my shoulder. "Sorry, Vi. I know you don't like talking about… And anyway, we're here to have fun."

"That's right." Finley's arm circle's my waist, not so subtly tugging me away from Grayson. "Vi, why don't we get you another drink."

But I'm still caught on two little words. "Every day?"

CHAPTER SEVEN

VIOLETTA AND I HAVEN'T SPOKEN since our day at the beach. Not even at her party a few days ago, where we maintained our old pattern: her, hardly caring I exist, and me, trying not to spend the entire night watching her laugh and drink and joke with others.

When Grayson admitted he'd told her about my visits to the hospital, he suggested I give her some space. But when I heard Violetta was feeling ill, nowhere to be seen at Karolina's birthday party, I didn't stop to think.

Now, waiting for her doorman to find out whether my presence will be tolerated, as my pulse races and palms sweat, my brain is finally starting to catch up. What if she just wanted a quiet evening? Or maybe some elite interpersonal politics are at play, and she isn't feeling ill at all.

But then, Violetta isn't one to miss a good party, and according to the photos already flooding the internet, Karolina's thirtieth would have put Gatsby's affairs to shame. Photos that did include Braxton.

So Violetta is almost certainly home alone.

The doorman nods and gestures toward the elevator. I stare at the lighted numbers that count the passing floors on the ride up. My knuckles hesitate a moment after their first rap on her door, then finally sound out an uneven rhythm. I can't hear any response within.

What was I thinking?

A click and a rustle swing her door open. Violetta's small frame is swallowed by the sweater she's wearing, and her hair rests in a messy knot at her neck. Outside the hospital, I've never seen her this pale.

"What are you doing here?"

All I want is to cradle her in my arms. Instead, I hold out the trite container of soup I brought for her. Her gaze flicks down to my outstretched hands, then back to me.

I let the soup drop a bit, finding the words to say, "I heard you weren't feeling well."

Her throat works, and her jaw tenses, her shoulders rounding a bit. Then coughs wrack her body, but she steps back, gesturing inside.

Slumped against the door, she watches me as she struggles to breathe. I set the soup on a small table just inside but don't dare to touch her. A part of me hates Braxton for leaving her alone to suffer like this; the other part is thrilled he isn't here.

"I'm not exactly up for entertaining," Violetta says between breaths.

But all I want is to be here for her. "I just thought you could use some company."

Adrian looks so earnest, and I don't have it in me to tell him to leave. Besides, if anything can convince him his claims of love are misplaced, it's my unfiltered reality.

"Make yourself comfortable," I murmur automatically. On my way to the open kitchen, I detour to shut the door to the converted second bedroom. Maybe not *entirely* unfiltered.

Pills lay piled beside a glass of water on the kitchen counter. I was trying to decide if I could stomach eating when the doorman called. Adrian hasn't moved, except to pick up the Styrofoam container again.

Another coughing fit brings him to my side, one hand reaching toward me. Only concern shows in his unexceptional brown eyes.

The container lands beside the pills.

"Chicken noodle soup," he says without my having to ask.

How perfectly normal, as if chicken soup really can fix anything. I turn to take down a bowl, and my hand comes away with two. He may as well stay, and I'm nothing if not a good hostess.

He pops the lid off the soup, then takes half a step toward the sink before asking, "May I?"

At my shrug, he plucks the ladle from its hook on the wall and doles out a portion of soup. A hint of steam rises from the bowl. He leaves the second one empty.

When I look up, a small line rests between his eyebrows.

"What is it?" I ask.

He hesitates a moment. "You should take the enzymes."

He's not wrong, but him recognizing the pills prickles discomfort along my skin. Grayson assured me Adrian isn't a stalker, but still. Even my lovers I keep as far away from my illness as possible, not that any of them have objected. They might pay for my treatments, but they don't need to know the details. William wouldn't know what these pills are for even if they were still in their bottles.

The last thing I need to have around is someone obsessed with my condition.

Adrian doesn't press the issue, filling the second bowl. The emptied container *thunks* against the island. "Should I take these to the table?" he asks.

"The couch."

He nods and walks away with the bowls. I choke down the pills and follow him with a couple spoons. At least with Adrian, there's no need for me to be sexy, or even remotely appealing. On days like this, I couldn't be either even if I wanted to try.

Violetta is watching the soup as if it's lumpy three-day-old gruel. I'd do anything to help her feel better, but I'm not foolish enough to believe that's possible. The best I can do is be here.

Staring definitely won't help, so I force my eyes away. Lights gleam through the sheer curtains covering the windows on the other end of the room. An oval dining table with a twisted pedestal base, surrounded by curving, high-backed chairs, is set in front of the windows. Two doors interrupt the pale yellow of the wall to my right, and a gleaming oak entertainment center stands to my left, facing the other side of the corner sofa.

Violetta's curled on that part of the couch, watching me. At least the bowl cradled in her hands is no longer full.

"How's the soup?" I ask inanely.

"Why don't you try it and see?" Irritation underscores her question.

I slip a spoonful in my mouth. Mrs. Levinson's slightly salted broth is rumored to truly cure all ills, and it's the best I've tasted, though I'd claim otherwise to my mother. Even better is seeing Violetta eat some more. It takes me almost no time to finish my portion, but she doesn't seem to have much of an appetite tonight.

"Would you like to watch something?" The entertainment center probably houses a TV, and I don't know what else to say. Any ease of conversation we had out on the beach has vanished entirely, but then that's understandable with Violetta not feeling well.

"As I said, I'm not up"—she swallows back a cough—"for entertaining." She slides her not-quite-emptied bowl onto the coffee table, her eyes lightly squinted from the pain.

"I'm sorry. Would you like me to go?" What else could I offer her besides freedom from me?

Her inhale ends with another bout of coughing, and she twists away, plucking a tissue from the end table beside her. Her small frame shakes, shoulders curling in over her torso. Before I know it, my hand is on her back. The tremors shake through my palm, and my jaw clenches as my own breath stills.

When the cough finally lets up, her shoulder blade presses into my palm as her lungs pull in air. The hand with the tissues drops from her mouth, and she turns her head just barely to look at me.

A faint sheen makes her eyes shine, but she blinks it away and forces her lips into a poor parody of a smile.

Belatedly I lift my hand, but can't yet force myself to move away. "Or, maybe I could read to you," I offer, hating the idea of leaving her even more now that I'm here.

She holds my gaze for a few more pounding heartbeats, then her chin wobbles unevenly up and down. Her eyes flick to my arm, still hovering behind her back. I shift away to my earlier spot on the sofa, and she slumps back with a tiny sigh, closing her eyes.

Unobserved, I clench my jaw against the nausea of seeing her suffer, stifling the urge to gulp in air myself.

When Violetta's eyes open, my features slip into as close to a poker face as I can manage. "Any preference?" I ask, as if the book is what matters. Although, I haven't seen any books in her apartment.

She leans forward to pick up a tablet I hadn't noticed from the coffee table, then flips the soft cover open and hands it to me, its screen displaying her digital shelves.

It doesn't take long for Violetta's eyes to drift shut again as I read. Sometimes her breath hitches, and I know she's fighting another bout of bone-shaking cough. It takes everything I have to read on as if I haven't noticed.

When my false lack of concern is about to slip, I take a sip from the glass of water she insisted on getting for me.

Barely focused on the words before me, I strain to hear her breathing. Forty-seven digital pages in, the stream of air has settled into a limping pattern. I let the tablet drift to my lap, pausing as I listen. She doesn't say anything.

Her head rests back on the couch, lips slightly parted. Pain occasionally twitches her features, but her unevenly steady breath doesn't change. The shadowed outline of her bed stands beyond the open bedroom door. Leaving her on the couch is not an option.

Should I wake her, or carry her?

My heart speeds at the thought of holding her close, if only to help her into her room. Into bed. The hammering echoes through my chest. Even knowing how ridiculous it is, I'm amazed she can't hear the beat in the otherwise silent apartment.

After setting the tablet aside, I stand. Violetta doesn't stir. Waking her from the relative comforts of sleep seems cruel, but is taking her into my arms also taking advantage?

I lose track of time as I stand, watching her, stuck in indecision. My heart pounds on. A light sheen of sweat coats my palms. I scrub them against the fabric of my pants.

I can't keep stalling, and in truth there isn't any question. I'd rather apologize for carrying her than for causing her pain, even the pain caused by waking her.

Lifting her is heartbreakingly easy, her delicate frame barely registering in my arms. Her head rests lightly on my shoulder. I want to hold her forever, as if my embrace could protect her from the ruthlessness of reality. But the harshest reality lies within her body, not the outside world.

Stepping carefully, I make my way to the bedroom. Briefly, my body blocks it from the living room's light. With the curtains drawn, the dark feels absolute. Another step and light seeps through, outlining the main pieces of furniture within.

Tenderly as I can, I kneel on the edge of her bed, laying her down toward the middle. My hands slip out from under her in a parting caress. I start to move away, but her hand finds mine despite the darkness, her fingers squeezing gently. Her eyes flutter open, and nothing could make me deny her silent request.

I twist from my kneeling position to sit on the bed, leaving my hand in hers. A moment later, the soft pinch of her fingers lessens. I shift our hands to take hers fully in mine, skimming my thumb over her knuckles. Her eyes disappear behind her eyelids, and she draws in a deeper breath, relaxing with the exhale as sleep lets her drift away.

﹏ CHAPTER EIGHT ﹏

I WOULD HAVE THOUGHT Adrian would stick around last night. Not that it matters. Maybe now his naive insistence on love will fade.

More importantly, I need to drag myself out of bed, deal with my morning treatment, and make it to Zumba. Or maybe yoga. Or maybe just a leisurely walk on my treadmill. Even making it into the room next door feels like a stretch today.

But my body's begging for some help, and Greenfield's already threatened to lock me away in the hospital again if things get worse. Fun as that sounds…

I shove my comforter off and sit up, looking around for my phone. It isn't on the bed or the nightstand. Yet another reason to get up.

My hair's a disaster, the tangled mess weighing heavier than normal, but no one's around to see, so I just twist it back. Brushing it can wait.

It isn't until I make it to the coffee table that I see him, lying compactly on the couch. Like even asleep, Adrian can't encroach on too much space, despite his height. What should I make of him being here? Maybe he was too exhausted to find his way home.

I should wake him, tell him to leave. But instead, I snatch my phone as it starts buzzing against the table. His head rolls toward the sound.

We missed you! reads the message from Finley, with a photo from Karolina's party. A great party and me—we're practically synonymous, and that isn't a coincidence. I should glance through the posted photos, wish Karolina a happy birthday on a couple sites. My phone vibrates again, and another text pops up. *Late lunch today?*

Definitely, I text back before pushing open the door to the converted second bedroom. Delicious gossip, that's sure to help me feel more like myself than working out ever could.

It takes me a minute to remember Adrian is still on my couch. No one ever spends the night here. James first rented this place for me, five years ago. It was a bit of a stretch for him, but a girl has to start somewhere. When I told Hari I didn't want to lose the rooms I'd come to think of as home, he bought the apartment outright and put the paperwork in my name. And even he didn't spend the night here.

To be fair, my lovers' homes have always been much more lavish than mine. But I'm plenty comfortable here, and when I'm not, I can go just about anywhere I want.

What I want now is for Adrian to leave.

A useless cough rips at my insides, and I stumble to the couch, gripping it for balance.

Maybe not entirely useless, since it wakes my lingering not-quite-guest.

Adrian sits up instantly. Mercifully, the cough itself is short-lived. I round the edge of the couch to sink onto it. Adrian watches me warily.

"You should go," I tell him.

He freezes for a prolonged moment, not even blinking, then finally nods, pushing up onto his feet. "How are you feeling?"

My face pulls into its habitual nonchalant smile. Even those muscles protest today. "I'll be fine."

❧ CHAPTER NINE ❧

"WHAT ARE YOUR PLANS TODAY?" William asks Monday morning, looking at me in the mirror as he straightens his tie.

Everything in his bedroom is in a sleek combination of grays—like his eyes—except the blue dress caught on a charcoal dresser. It'll be far too wrinkled to wear home. The walk of shame is beyond low-class, but that's why half his closet is filled with my clothes. He may not spend the night at my place, but I spend plenty of nights here.

I prop up on my elbows to see him better. "The party plans need some finishing touches."

His eyes refocus on his own reflection. When he turns around, he's impeccably dressed, the consummate professional—refined, meticulous, and in control. "Would you like me to call a car for you?"

He used to bring me breakfast in bed. But this is what happens when a relationship settles down in a routine. It becomes comfortable, no longer pressured to prove itself. *Stagnates* is another word.

"Sure." I swing my legs over the side of the bed, turning away from him. "Thank you."

"There's no rush, of course." His loafers appear in the corner of my vision, stepping toward me, and then his knuckles brush my cheek.

I tilt my head back, meeting his gaze with an easy smile. "An hour will be fine."

"Good." His hand lingers a moment before he steps back.

My smile fades to neutral as he moves away, out of sight. That's what we are with each other, now—pleasantly neutral.

"Oh, I wanted to warn you," he says.

I twist to see his hand already on the doorknob. Arching my back draws his eyes briefly down the bare line.

"I won't be able to make it to the opera tomorrow night," he continues a moment later. "But the box is at your disposal."

"All right." I attend for the performance, not the body beside mine.

But he takes my lack of argument as displeasure, and an indulgent half-smile stretches his cheeks. "I'll make it up to you. Come by afterward?"

"Of course." At the end of the day, I can't fault him for needing to work late. After all, his work pays for my pleasures.

Chapter Ten

THE ONE THING I HAVE GOING for me is that I'm good at my job. Or I used to be, when I could focus—when seeing Violetta from afar filled my nights or the odd weekend event, and yearning for her could be neatly relegated to those times. Now that I've actually spent time with her, spoken with her, held her... My mind strays to her constantly.

Even though I haven't heard from her. The thin pretense I had showing up at her door last week didn't exactly allow for a follow-up, especially after her dismissal the next morning.

Her first large party is next weekend, and I imagine Grayson will let me tag along. But that's ten days away. Normally I'd throw myself into my work.

Coffee. That has to help. I can't afford to be fired.

The break room is blissfully empty, sparing me from small talk. Better yet, the coffee pot is fairly full.

Half a cup later, I'm finally making some progress, so unsurprisingly my phone buzzes. I flip it over on autopilot, still scanning the latest instructions from my boss on my desktop's screen. When I glance down to the smaller phone screen, I nearly spit out the coffee I just sipped.

> Rigoletto tonight. Join me? Meet there at 7 if you're interested.

The message isn't the shocking part—the sender is. It's possible the text was misaddressed, but otherwise, at the very least, I have to have crossed her mind. I don't dare think she's asking me out, but the text is unmistakably an invitation to escort her tonight, which implies she enjoys my company. Or had no other options, but for Violetta? That would never be the case.

One thing's for sure: I won't get any more work done today.

The last time I was at the Lincoln Center was also the first time I said more than *hello* to Violetta. Now, the rush of operagoers around me slows as I catch sight of her. Against the red backdrop of the Metropolitan Opera's lobby, she's impossible to miss. In a short gold shimmer that somehow draws attention to her waist, with glittering detail crossing over her chest and up to one shoulder, she's resplendent. Her hair is gathered entirely up, baring the line of her neck. I can't imagine anything on stage tearing my eyes away from her tonight.

I'm nearly at her side before she notices me, and then she smiles, throwing off the rhythm of my heart. "Hello, Adrian."

"Violetta. Thank you for the invitation." Her gaze starts to move away from me, but I add, "Braxton couldn't make it?"

Her eyes flick back to me. "He's working late."

I nod as if spending an evening out with her is commonplace, as if Braxton's absence isn't life changing. "I'm glad you're feeling better."

Her head tilts gently in acknowledgement, but then she straightens abruptly, her features settling into a broader smile. "Ah! There they are."

Striding toward us, Grayson extends a flute of champagne to Violetta. Greenfield is at his side, frowning.

"You better take this," Violetta says, seamlessly shifting the champagne in my direction, eyes trained on Greenfield. "Before the good doctor has a stroke."

I take the glass reflexively, still trying to catch up.

"Adrian!" Grayson exclaims softly, expression straining to hold back his amusement. He gulps the tawny liquor in his own glass, draining half of it at once. "Didn't expect to see you here tonight."

The growing weight in my chest makes it difficult to speak. I sip the champagne, as if the blockage could be so easily cleared. "I was grateful for the invitation. Doctor,"—I turn away from the laughter in my friend's eyes—"good to see you again."

"And you. How lucky that we both get to benefit from Violetta's generosity." He says it without a trace of sarcasm.

But Violetta has said it herself: she does everything for pleasure. I doubt the simple fact of our company is her sole goal in inviting us all.

As if to drive the edge of disappointment home, Prudence brushes Violetta's shoulder, grinning with false delight. "You naughty thing! Snatching three handsome men all to yourself. What will William say when he finds out?"

Violetta answers, but the pounding in my veins saves me from hearing. How idiotic, thinking I was the only one she had invited, that it was *my* presence here that mattered. No, she wanted me here tonight at most to make her message clear: I am but one of many admirers to her, and she is far beyond any of our grasps except when her *generosity* gifts us with her attention.

To me, everyone else fades into the background. But to her, I will never stand out from the blur of bodies drawn to her shining star.

Adrian has been moody all evening. He didn't even attempt to protest when Grayson slid into the seat beside mine. So much for his claims of love.

I should be relieved, but I'm annoyingly unsettled. I'm wanted by nearly every man in our circle—in Manhattan *and* abroad—even if they all know I'm taken.

Then again, none of those men have ever seen me disheveled and in old sweats, and this is precisely why.

Looking flawless, the furtive looks in my direction, being both desired and out of their reach—it's just another of life's pleasures. I certainly didn't dress for Adrian's sake tonight. Just as well, since he barely looked at me during the intermission.

Maybe *Rigoletto* wasn't to his taste, though tonight's performance was great, the costumes exquisite. And of course the titular character was terrific as well. The cheers echoing through the opera house are well deserved.

"Outstanding!" Greenfield comments as we make our way from our seats. Our group stalls in the lobby, and he inclines his head. "Violetta, thank you again for the invitation."

"As I hope this proved," I tease, "New York has more to offer than the hospital."

Greenfield smiles at the jab, but then this is a topic we've discussed at length, since his lack of social life is much easier to fix than my body. "Nevertheless," he says, expression slipping to professional concern, "I'll see you tomorrow."

"I wouldn't dare miss it." Maybe inviting him into my world was a mistake. He would have no trouble tracking me down if I do decide to skip the appointment. Other doctors would just bill me—well, William—for a no-show fee, but Greenfield would probably call me himself.

As if reading my thoughts, he narrows his eyes. Whatever's on his mind, though, he keeps it to himself, turning to Grayson and his friend. "Gentlemen. I should get going, but I trust you'll take good care of Miss Dorée."

"She's in some of the best hands in the city," Grayson goads with a crooked smile.

Adrian murmurs a goodbye, and the doctor soon disappears into the exiting crowd.

"Where are we off to next, then?" Grayson asks. "Vi, care for a nightcap?"

Adrian's jaw clenches. He's watching me now, oddly intense.

For show more than anything, I resettle William's latest gift on my wrist. Adrian's gaze stalls on my torso, near the movement, and that itch of my irritation lessens a bit.

"Not tonight, I'm afraid," I answer to Grayson's invitation.

"Can I escort you home?" Adrian offers instantly.

A soft chuckle escapes me. "I'm not going home."

It takes a moment, but understanding finally reaches his expression, crumbling the edges of his hopefulness. He blinks a few times, quickly, then nods once.

I almost regret reminding him of William, but his reaction is further proof that my life has no place for him. The reality of my practical relationships would crush his fanciful notions of romance. Let him find his love with a woman who's capable of it. Neutral luxury suits me just fine.

"Don't tell me," Grayson says as Violetta's car drives off, "the curse is finally broken."

"What curse?" I head toward the subway, and he falls into step beside me.

"Your obsession. You've been positively dour all night." He slings his suit jacket over one shoulder. "I would have thought you'd be thrilled."

"Thrilled? To be part of a mass invitation? Or, worse." I stop, turning to him as a realization hits me. "Did you suggest she invite me?"

"No." He stretches the syllable out as if I'm missing the point. "Which is exactly why you should be over the moon. A month ago, Vi didn't know you existed. Now she's inviting you to hang out."

"Among any number of other men."

"Not any number, Braxton only buys the one box." The teasing falls flat. At my frown, Grayson's lips slip into a wry smile. His free hand lands on my shoulder. "Don't forget, of all the men in New York, Violetta Dorée just chose to spend her night with you. And it's not like she doesn't have her pick."

"Like you and Greenfield."

Grayson starts back down the street, and a few steps later I move too, catching up. "Don't kid yourself," he says. "Both the doctor and I are closer to her usual style. And anyway, she won't be leaving Braxton any time soon." At my silence, he adds, "But not that long ago, your bourgeois little heart would have burst at the mere possibility of her knowing your name. Don't discount your progress."

I can't read the expression on his profile, though the street isn't all that dark. But he isn't wrong, and I can't help the flicker of hope that grows at his insistence that her invitation did matter. That she really did want my company tonight. Which is a start.

"Since when did you decide to encourage me?" I ask eventually.

He glances at me with a grin. "It's entertaining, that's all. Maybe I don't want the show to end."

I can't hold his gaze. I've considered before that I may be nothing more than a social experiment to him. Apparently my confidence is easily shaken tonight.

"Or maybe," Grayson says, "I hate seeing you this hopelessly miserable."

And maybe, even my habitually cynical friend actually wants to believe in the possibilities of love.

<h1 style="text-align:center">❦ CHAPTER ELEVEN ❦</h1>

MY NUMBERS ARE DOWN. I guess since we're comparing to when I was living in the sheltered care of the hospital, that's to be expected. Greenfield is worried, as his job dictates he must be. He wants me to increase my daily treatments, but with my comeback party just over a week away and the summer season ramping up, I can't imagine having the time.

Granted, everything is on track with the party. At a certain point, it's all about knowing the best locations and the best caterers, and having ideas for an intriguing theme that hits the right balance of opulence, and then everyone will be happy. I may have lost time in the hospital, but I haven't forgotten how to bring together a flawless event.

The only piece left unfinished is the guest list. Oh, everyone knows when and where the party will be. What they don't know is who's invited.

And because of my time out of the loop, I'm meeting Finley later for a mani/pedi to finally catch up on the latest scandals. But with some time to spare, a champagne-and-pearl body treatment sounds heavenly right now, to de-stress after Greenfield's drab office and all his frowns.

Something tells me William won't mind indulging me. To be fair, he probably won't even look at the bill.

I slide into the black car already waiting for me and direct the driver to the spa. Lucky me that I don't have to call ahead for an appointment.

The moment I step into the earth-toned lobby, I can practically feel the tension melt from my body in anticipation of the pampering to come.

Chapter Twelve

"YOU'VE OUTDONE YOURSELF," William says the night of my big event, stepping up behind me as guests trickle in.

He's not wrong, but like everyone, William knows nothing of tonight's surprise. I wonder how he'll react, whether he'll participate. I somehow can't imagine it, but maybe the atmosphere will encourage him to experiment.

The night's just beginning, and already the open space is filled with the unmistakable chatter of a good time. Every version of a high-fashion toga imaginable swirls through the room, lit by an almost absurd number of column-shaped candles set in woven ivy wreaths, as well as by purple and pink spotlights pointed at the walls. Unobtrusive waitstaff circulate bite-sized Greek delicacies, though a full buffet is arranged for later.

This evening will be talked about everywhere, whether it succeeds or fails. Of course, failure isn't an option.

"So what's the big secret?" Prue asks, appearing before us in a dress with barely enough material to be called a toga. A golden wreath decorates her chocolate hair.

"Secret?" William echoes. No surprise that the socialites will have heard more gossip than him. The toga I chose suits him well, the white fabric trimmed with purple embroidery and gathered at his left shoulder with a golden pin I found. It drapes down to his calves and covers most of his chest, but still reveals the breadth of his shoulders. Powerful yet proper.

"No spoilers," I tell them both, a rush of adrenaline tinged with anxiety flowing through me.

"You're evil," Prue quips, before being distracted by the arrival of Della, in a short, off-the-shoulder white dress paired with golden laces twining up her legs to mid-thigh. A brief hello later, she pulls Prue away to whine about her latest tabloid scandal.

Finley finds me then, with her latest beau in tow—an ambassador, I think, more than twice her age, but then William is nearly twice mine. He soon melts into the crowd to fill his role as host, greeting our guests. So far, everything is going smoothly.

The majority of people seem to have arrived, though I haven't yet seen Adrian. Or Grayson, or a handful of others.

In any case, there's time for everyone to sink into the revelry before I reveal tonight's surprise.

It hits me as I hand the doorman my personally addressed invitation to Violetta's Bacchanalia-inspired party: in terms of Manhattan's social scene, I've finally arrived. It's the first time I merited my own invitation rather than hanging on to Grayson's.

If only I knew what that actually meant.

Aside from the little card, I haven't seen or heard from Violetta since she drove off from the opera. I have no right to be jealous, and in so many ways I'm not. What she has with Braxton is empty, but even the superficial ways in which he knows her, can be with her… I thought I wanted any time she would give me, but these last few weeks, the desire for so much more, for everything we could have together, has inundated me.

With Grayson busy showing off his costume, I make my way around the edges of the room, watching Violetta's guests indulge in an event that thankfully doesn't quite reach the standard set by the ancients. At least not yet. Although, limiting the lighting to mostly candles does help lower any inhibitions those in attendance may still have.

I don't catch sight of Violetta herself until she calls for the room's attention. My mouth goes dry as blood pounds through my head. Intricate white braids cover her torso, and seemingly endless material floats around her legs, a dangerously high slit playing peekaboo with her every move. Her hair falls in waves around her shoulders, gleaming in the candlelight. Even her skin seems to shimmer, as if dusted with gold. For all I know, that may in fact be the case.

My hand snatches the first filled glass it finds as I drink in the sight of her. She teases some surprise addition to tonight's festivities, her lips stretching into a brilliant smile. Her gaze sweeps around the guests gathered before her, and as it pauses for the briefest moment on me, everything stills. Whatever questions I might have about the meaning of her invitation, Grayson was right. She notices me now.

A small voice in my mind whispers a thought that sparks a flash of hope: does she actually care I'm here?

Everything came together fabulously. The painting room is pristine, for now. White drapery hides, and protects, the walls. Strategically placed paint supplies lie in wait—everything from bowls and brushes, to delicate paint balls, to hidden automated misters that will infuse the room with powdered bursts of color at pre-timed intervals.

Tittering joins speculation as everyone filters inside. Wait-staff circulate with golden cloth bags for any irreplaceable jewelry or cell phones. Waterproof lining will protect their contents, and woven handles can be looped over a wrist or tied to a belt, so everyone can embrace the revelry about to fill the room. I hope.

That's one of the unseen pressures of a reputation like mine—maintaining the gradually increasing standard for my events, all without any repeats.

I call for everyone's attention, and over a hundred curious expressions face me. "Fair warning," I say, flashing them a mischievous smile, "everyone in this room *will* soon be transformed. For anyone who doesn't want to participate in the fun, you have the next thirty seconds to return to the ballroom."

Of course, no one but the waiters makes a move to leave, worried about missing out. My gaze sweeps the crowd, seeking anyone who looks like they want to bolt. Grayson in his bare-chested toga smirks at me, ignoring Finley, Prue, Karolina, and Della whispering beside him. Adrian hovers off to the side, alone. Hari looks around as his latest girl fondles his chest, desperately marking her territory. Nisha and Clara sidle casually closer to a cluster of financiers. William's caught close to the center of the room, his jaw clenched, but he'll stick it out, much as he hates being unprepared—and getting messy. With colleagues and clients here, he can't be one to back down. He might be annoyed later that I didn't warn him, but then the spontaneity is part of why he likes having me around.

"Five, four…" As I count, an excited chatter builds from the back of the room. I catch the eye of the last remaining server, standing unobtrusively by the masked switch. "One."

A half-second of hushed anticipation fills the air, then bursts with the first surge of color. At the delighted smiles, my own anxiety releases as well.

But a familiar tightness in my chest persists.

With everyone distracted, I slip outside, taking only a few steps before a cough rips from my throat. It seems to echo through the ballroom, empty now except for the staff.

I bury the sound behind one palm while the other presses into the wall to keep me upright.

A warm hand lands on my elbow, the firm grip helping me fight the shaking. I try to pull away, to stifle the cough, which of course only makes it worse. The hold lessens, and Adrian comes into view, eyebrows drawn together with his worry. His body blocks me from the room, saves me from any prying eyes, and I strive to pull in air, sheltered between him and the wall.

The moment of my reprieve, I move toward a secluded alcove at the back of the room. Adrian shadows me, his hand coming to my back, landing discretely on the straps of my dress. He leads me to one of the armchairs, and I sink onto the plush brocade as a smaller cough comes from my throat.

He disappears a moment but soon offers me a glass of raspberry water. Rather than take it, I lean into the chair, closing my eyes as I finally catch my breath.

"Violetta," Adrian says quietly. When I open my eyes, he's crouched beside me.

"You can call me Vi, you know," I say for lack of anything better.

"Vi," he repeats, as if testing the sound of the familiarity. In the dim light, his nearly bare chest doesn't look half bad. Plenty of women here tonight would likely show an interest in him, if he didn't hide on the outskirts.

I sit up a bit straighter. "Your toga has no color." Maybe the lighter topic will remind him of the delights available beyond this disconnected not-quite-room.

"Same goes for yours," he answers, still far too serious.

"Oh, I'll join the fun in a minute or two. You don't have to wait for me." It sounds like a conversation we've had before.

He stands but doesn't move away, ignoring my practiced assurances. "I prefer your company, if you don't mind."

Impeccably tactful, how he skirts the reason I was pulled away. "You'd have much more fun out there." Another, thankfully shorter, coughing fit completes my point.

Adrian waits silently until it ends. Of course, he's seen me looking worse. His jaw shifts pensively to one side when I look up at him, as though he's holding something back. I raise my eyebrows rather than speak, but he doesn't need more blatant prompting.

"You know," he says slowly, "for a supposed hedonist, you have an incredibly strong masochistic streak."

❧ CHAPTER THIRTEEN ❧

I DON'T KNOW WHAT MADE ME SAY IT, though the thought had been bouncing around my head awhile. Watching her suffering, killing herself to maintain the charade of an endlessly carefree life, surrounded by people who clearly don't care for her welfare beyond the illusion…

She considers me for a prolonged moment before standing and smoothing her skirt. "So I'm a failure as a hedonist, then?" There's an alluring challenge in her eyes.

I hold her gaze, adding, "Especially since you intentionally avoid life's greatest pleasures."

Humor softens her lips and her stance. "And according to you, those would be?"

"An amazing, soul-deep conversation. Laughter shared over a delicious home-cooked meal. Cuddling up with a beautiful, evocative book, or movie. And so many others, including the one you've asked me not to mention."

"Love," Vi scoffs. "You talk about love as if it's the solution to everything, as if it's more important than anything else."

"Like what, four-hundred-dollar facials?" I counter, my concern spilling out as sarcasm.

Her eyes narrow. "Like financial security. Like quality healthcare, and yes, the luxuries as well—the gourmet food, and the massages, and the beautiful clothes, and the trips around the world."

I know I shouldn't say it, but I can't stop myself, desperate to get through to her. "But you don't take advantage of the finest healthcare money can buy, do you?"

She backs slightly, chin notching up. "I choose to live my life, enjoy everything I can about it, rather than sacrifice it to managing a disease that's fatal anyway. Who are you to judge me for that?"

"I'm not. I'm not judging you." My palms lift with my helplessness. "I just can't stand to see you suffer."

"No one's asking you to watch." She spins away, stepping over to the window.

All I can say is, "Vi, please."

Her head turns an inch or so toward me, but she continues looking out into the night.

I swallow down my doubt. "I want you to be happy. I want you to have the finest of everything, but I also want you to feel well enough to actually enjoy it, rather than being holed up in a dark room during your own party, or being even more ill tomorrow because you overexerted yourself tonight." I pause, but she doesn't move.

It hits me, then, that this may be the last time I ever see her. Whether she decides I'm not worth having around, or simply because I can't keep watching her do this to herself when modern medicine could add years—*good* years—to her life, the result will be the same.

I step closer, leaving her just out of reach. "I can't give you everything Braxton can—not the diamonds or the box seats, or the fancy gowns. But you've had those, you've experienced that side of life."

Her head turns a bit further, pauses, then moves enough that we lock eyes.

"Let me show you what it's like to be loved, to be cherished."

Her lashes brush her cheeks.

"I promise," I whisper, suddenly hoarse. "We will be comfortable, and we will eat delicious food, and I will find plenty to entertain you. And I will prioritize *you*, not the picture you make at my side."

Her gaze drops, a tiny crinkle appearing between her brows.

"Please." I move back, popping the intense bubble that built around us as I spoke. "Give yourself the chance to experience a life Braxton's money could never buy you."

Give us a chance, my heart begs as I walk away.

Adrian is wrong, of course; I have known love.

I have seen love destroy the very people who felt it, who were crushed by the reality of my condition, of my life. People I love, who are so much better off without me, and my treatments, and my bills.

It might be different, romantic love. Adrian would say I couldn't know. But wouldn't it only be worse? More intense, and ultimately so much more destructive.

And yet, Adrian is not like my family, beaten down by expenses they never asked for, worn away by concern and fear, by everything my life was before I came here. Is it fair to convince myself he'd know what he's getting into, even while I know how far from true that is?

The entire thing is out of the question, of course. Adrian may not understand, but I do love my life, this world, my friends. And William suits me well enough for now.

Still, I can't help but remember how thoughtful Adrian was, reading to me, carrying me to bed, not leaving me as my traitorous body tortured me. That part of my life will always stay hidden from my friends, even as they're all aware of its inevitable end.

They sent balloons, and the less thoughtful candy, as I lay in the hospital. But other than a couple brief visits from Grayson, even William didn't set foot in the place after checking me in.

Except Adrian. Had he really visited every day? And why do I find that charming rather than a bit odd? We hadn't even spoken then.

What would be the point, anyway, of opening up to his supposed love, when an inevitable expiration date awaits? Why give up the countless pleasures easily procured with the swipe of a card? It would be unbelievably stupid.

For what? The illusion of some fairytale notion of love being all anyone really needs? What else could I be to Adrian other than a conquest, a prize to be claimed, same as to any other man I've been with. His social standing in this world would soar, or maybe mine would plummet to obscurity. Or both. Leaving me with nothing but false, foolish promises.

What is love if not an immense risk with indeterminable rewards at best? Only an idiot would choose it over a stream of luxuries sprinkled atop the security of stability.

Violetta Dorée may be many things, but I am not an idiot.

CHAPTER FOURTEEN

"GOT YOU!" FINLEY TEASES, dropping a handful of paintballs near my feet minutes after I rejoin the party in the color room. Blues and yellows decorate my hemline, and I laugh, clinking my champagne flute against hers.

Della runs past, chased by a blur of color that is likely responsible for the hand-shaped splotches on her hips. Other couples have retreated to the corners or sought out secluded spots, lending their entwined bodies to the ambiance.

"You are entirely too pristine," Prue announces, giggling as she slides her arm around Finley's shoulders. Swirls of paint cover her from head to perfectly lacquered toe.

Noticing our group, Nisha swoops in as well. "Did you see Raban going at it with Clara? How long do you think it'll be before he gets her to go blonde?"

"Oh, you are woefully behind," Finley says with her all-knowing smile.

"We should do brunch tomorrow, you can catch us all up," Prue suggests. Her eyes follow a tray of hors d'oeuvres passing just outside the painting room. "Add in a spin class, so we can work off all this decadence."

"To be truly decadent," I point out, "you can't worry about the consequences."

A mix of giggles and groans meets the statement.

"Besides," Finley adds, "Vi always disappears right after her parties."

"Oh, that's right." Nisha's purple-lined eyes train on me. "Where *do* you go to celebrate your latest triumph?"

"More importantly, how do we get you to make an exception?" Finley asks. I would have thought she knew better.

"Sorry, ladies. A girl has to have some secrets." In my case, many. I flash them all a smile along with a calculated lift of my eyebrows.

A few feigned pouts later, they're on to firming up their plans.

It's a surprising struggle to maintain my pleasant expression. How have I never noticed how much of my life I keep hidden from my friends? Protecting them from my reality with the half-truths and deflections they never even try to look beyond. What would they say if they knew the price I pay for draining nights like this one?

But willful ignorance is integral to our fun; it wouldn't do for reality to intrude. After all, that's the life I prefer as well.

This entire lavish culture is the ideal escape, temporary as it may be, from the harsh truth of my health. And it sure beats the nonstop concern and hyper-focus of people who see nothing more to me than my condition.

The flashing neon sign that was my illness finally disappeared when I found this haze of hedonism. The growing group around me doesn't think twice about needling me to relent and join their evolving plans.

But that's just it—they don't think twice.

Chapter Fifteen

Grayson grunts at the morning light, pouring brandy into his mug before swinging the decanter in my direction.

"It's barely ten," I point out, but he just shrugs, sips his spiked coffee, and leans back with a moan.

I stare at the black brew a moment, then reach for the brandy.

Grayson's eyes focus for the first time as he watches. "Okay, what don't I remember?"

The bite of the alcohol or maybe the comment makes me grimace. I haven't actually told him about my pathetic pleas to Violetta. What will I do if I never hear from her again?

"For someone who finally arrived last night, you're downright gloomy."

Rather than answer, I top my mug off with more liquor.

"What did the big, bad Vi do?" He throws his arm around my shoulders, jostling me on the couch. "Come on, you can tell me."

Silence stretches out between us as my mind tries to process everything that's happened, that went wrong. Grayson lets go and splashes more brandy into his nearly empty mug.

"I've lost her," I finally say.

"Don't be ridiculous. She was never yours to lose." He says it casually, as though the whole thing is inconsequential.

To him, maybe it is. To Vi, too, probably.

But everything that could have been taunts me as it slips away.

Alone in my apartment, I don't have to pretend. The coughing, the mucus, the treatments, the pills. The pain. No one's around to stare worriedly or talk about me in hushed tones, as if my condition is a secret I don't know. No one's there to care that without expertly applied makeup, I actually *look* sick. Last night took a lot out of me, I guess.

But the photos on my stream are filled with color and grins, and hefty speculation fills the comments. Definitely a successful night.

Grayson pops up on my screen, with two painted women on either side and a full glass of wine lifted toward the camera— a great image of Bacchus for the night. I could call him, but he'd want to go out, or drink, and probably both. Not that I blame him, of course. Doing what you want with your time is the prerogative of the shamelessly wealthy.

As if to underscore the point, a selfie of Finley, Prue, and a couple others pops up with a chime. *Come out of hiding and join us!!* the caption reads. I toss the phone away, and it bounces softly on the bed. Like always, the blank ceiling offers no comfort. Maybe I should have it painted. There's no shortage of talented starving artists in New York who could use a temporary patron.

But that does nothing to help me today. The blend of boredom and exhaustion is no less annoying despite its familiarity.

Blindly, I pull open the top drawer of my bedside table, fumbling around inside until my fingers snag the rubber edge of my tablet cover. Later, maybe I'll make it out to the living room and the pricey flat screen, but this will have to do for now. Pulling my eyes open, I flip off the cover and tap the first audiobook on my list.

But as the narrator starts speaking, the voice I hear is Adrian's. I feel the strength of his hold as he carries me to bed, sets me down ever so gently.

Every man I've been with since I came to New York has cared for me, of course, providing me with anything a girl could want. They've held me, too, as we found pleasure in each other's arms.

Adrian's embrace is different, somehow. Giving, undemanding—unlike his declarations.

Let me show you what it's like to be cherished.

Reciprocity is a requirement of love, but of companionship?

These times alone I save as a break from the everyday opulence of my life. A life to which Adrian is the perfect antithesis.

Grayson had to double-check I wasn't seeing things when Violetta's text popped up on my phone. Not the most reliable verification system, sure, but at least he had no reason to hallucinate the exact same message.

Come over?

Succinct, direct, and yet endlessly mysterious. No one sees Violetta after her big parties, no doubt due to the extreme toll on her body. *Vi.* Even in my mind, the diminutive feels overly familiar, despite her blunt permission. Whether she's decided in my favor or just wants to scoff at me some more, all I can think of is seeing her again. I was kidding myself yesterday, thinking I could walk away. Of course I can't—wouldn't, even if she never returns my feelings, never prioritizes taking care of herself over the whirlwind life of a socialite.

The doorman checks something on the desk then sends me up without calling. When silence greets my knock, my heart sinks. Should I have taken the time to respond while rushing over here? Had she meant the message for someone else? Or worse, was she lying inside, in pain or even—

Vibration against my leg pulls me away from the crushing image in my mind, and I slip my phone out, ready for Grayson's sarcastic commentary. Two new words are there instead. Following their implied invitation, I twist the knob, and the door swings open to an empty room.

"Violetta?" I call once inside, then clear my throat. "Vi?"

Coughing echoes from her bedroom. I hover in the entry-way, glancing around for any way to bring her comfort. She ignored the water I offered her last night, and besides a multi-colored puddle of fabric likely to be her dress from the party, nothing else catches my eye. Still, the coughing pulls me forward, step after step until I see her, curled in a pile of blankets on her bed.

❧ Chapter Sixteen ❧

ENERGY THRUMS THROUGH ME, the subdued dancing of my foot its only escape.

I don't know how I let this happen. How many nights has it been—how many times? I couldn't count, but I never spend my evenings or weekends alone now. Parties, nights out with William, or in with Adrian.

He's stopped his foolish talk of love, but there he always is, bringing me food or even cooking, reading to me or laughing at silly movies, like tonight. Whenever I don't feel up to going out, he's there, not just willing to keep me company but *happy* to, even out of sight of the social elite.

Oh, who am I kidding? Saturday I let Adrian take me home after the ballet. William was out of town, of course, and yet. There are bound to be rumors. *What is she thinking?* they'll whisper.

And the only answer I'll have is: *I don't know.*

He's sweet, though—nice. Not one comment on the mound of pills that should precede each meal, but his jaw clenches, clearly disapproving, any time I forget. No pretenses that I'm well, but no boxing me in as *sick*. How does he manage that? With him, I almost forget. And all without the late nights or flowing alcohol.

But still Greenfield was unhappy with me at today's appointment. My numbers keep slipping down. A frown pulls at my face, and I shake my head slightly to wipe my expression. No need for premature wrinkles. If I'm going to die young, it may as well be young and beautiful.

The couple on my TV kisses, and I glance beside me at Adrian. His head has fallen back against the couch, his eyes closed and lips parted. A hint of stubble covers his jaw, but since he visits after work, I almost never see him any other way. He'd rather spend that bit of time with me than waste it on appearances.

It's sloppy. And sweet.

As credits roll, I reach for the remote and shut off the TV. I should wake him, send him home, but there's still time before the last train. And if he leaves, I'll probably just fall into bed. Greenfield's threat of another hospitalization if I'm not more consistent with my treatments looms over me. Skipping tonight's would probably be a bad start.

A persistent hum greets the sharp inhale that jerks me out of sleep. The television's off, and Vi is no longer beside me on the couch. I fumble at my wrist, drawing back my sleeve to check the time. Late, but I can still make it home for a few hours' sleep instead of bumming around the station, waiting for the first morning train.

I can't believe I wasted this time with her, but the late nights must be getting to me. Of course, I wouldn't trade evenings with Vi for anything—definitely not for a bit more sleep. Or at least, not intentionally.

The humming hasn't stopped, and there are no other sounds of life. I scrub the remnants of sleep from my face then push up from the couch. For once the spare room's door isn't tightly shut, the room beyond it clearly lit. The humming comes from inside.

I clear the dishes to the kitchen before coming to the partially opened door. The brush of my knuckles pushes it just far enough that I can see Vi, and our eyes meet. Hers grow round, the plastic contraption in her mouth wobbling with her surprise before she resettles it. A bright-blue vest overwhelms her torso, vibrating her small frame to loosen the mucus clogging her lungs.

Her gaze still on me, I step into the small room with its pale-yellow walls and overstuffed furniture. A hose connects her vest to a machine the size of a carry-on suitcase. Her chin notches up in challenge, worry or fear filling her eyes.

I barely notice the steps it takes to reach her side, hating everyone in her life who never cared to support her. But she's let me in, finally, and I have no intention of leaving her. Perched on the edge of the armrest-less couch, I take her hand, interweaving our fingers, and squeeze lightly.

Her eyes close, head tilting back to rest on the pillow wedged behind her, but her hand stays wrapped in mine. And then she squeezes back.

I don't remember the last time someone saw me do my treatment. Years ago, for sure. Not since I left home, probably. That's the point of this room, locked at all times except when I'm inside. It's not chic, or fit for company. It's not a mess, either, but it's designed for comfort—as much as can be offered while my body shakes and coughs rip through me.

None of my lovers have been here. Granted, they rarely do more than hover inside the door, if they come up at all. William hasn't in ages.

The medical equipment travels with us, of course, fitting easily on the private jets and then in a corner of a hotel suite, tucked out of the way and promptly forgotten until it's loaded up again. Greenfield isn't wrong about my lack of compliance, but there are better things to do in the hours this requires, especially when surrounded by the sumptuousness of Europe, or even here in New York.

All of which feels impossibly far away as I take the nebulizer from my mouth and shut off the vest. I reach for the tissues automatically, holding my breath a moment before pushing it out in a rough cough. Adrian's fingers tighten in mine. Over and over, I force air through my lungs. The muscles over my ribs strain, already exhausted, the pitiful attempt to expel mucus wringing me dry.

The fingers of my free hand find the Velcro straps of the vest, tugging at them ineffectually. I pause, gathering myself for another attempt, but then Adrian moves, freeing me.

My eyes open to him standing above me, and I let him help me shrug out of the vest. His knuckles brush my cheek, exceedingly gentle. Then he bends and twists, slipping his arms beneath my knees and shoulders at once. My fingers curl into his sweater as he carries me to my bed. I don't let go as he sets me down. His face hovers above mine. Time stretches out as we stare at each other in the dark.

Tightening my grip, I lift myself up or maybe pull him down. His hands brace around me, one knee pressing into the mattress as his head ducks. And our lips finally meet.

The unassuming warmth soon lifts away. I tug him to the side, and he pushes his body over mine to land lightly on the bed. He watches me a moment, then lifts my hand from its place on his chest, maneuvering me into his arms. His lips press into my hair. With an exhale, my eyes drift shut.

Feeling his chest move against me with his breath, I can't help wonder… What would it be like to fall in love?

PART II

CHAPTER SEVENTEEN

"G'MORNING." ADRIAN SMILES up at me as I make my way down the stairs.

"Stop looking at me like that," I say, but my lips tug up as well. All these weeks, and that look of his hasn't changed. Appreciative. Devoted.

Happy.

An exhale matches my final step down.

Adrian pushes his laptop aside. "Are you hungry?"

I pull the cream from the fridge before pouring myself some coffee. "I'll just have a bagel," I tell him, turning around with the aromatic roast. "I want to get going."

He nods, then stands to clear his dishes from the table. He used to wait for me, but I couldn't stand it—knowing my treatments were holding up his day. Now our routine is simple. There's no bumping into each other or accidentally stepping in the other's way as I toast my bagel and grab the honey cream cheese while he takes care of his dishes.

My first bite is accompanied by the brush of his lips and scrape of his stubble on my cheek. I shake my head to clear off the dopey smile as his footsteps pad upstairs so he can shave before we go. It's easy, intimately cozy.

And amazing, how much I look forward to a simple bike ride down to the farmer's market and another day by the beach.

I love seeing Vi like this. Tendrils of hair whip around her face as we pedal toward our temporary home. Our lovers' getaway. The thought still makes me giddy, my heart flutter. Hard to believe it's been almost a month since we came out to the Hamptons. A bit longer since she officially left Braxton.

Vi glances over her shoulder at me then veers off the road toward our new favorite burger place. When she's gotten through her Nutella milkshake and most of her burger, she wipes the juices off her fingers and sighs in that contentedly full way, then snakes a sweet potato fry off my plate.

I grin, nudging the plate toward her across the laminated table, but she shakes her head, the humor edging her expression slipping away.

"What is it?" I ask after a sip of tart strawberry lemonade.

"I have to go see Greenfield tomorrow, go into the city." She shoves her own plate away then wraps her arms around her waist.

"Okay. We can spend one night away from our beach paradise," I tease, but she doesn't react. "I'll drive in with you," I offer. "You can see your friends afterward, and I can meet up with Grayson. We can get that Chinese food you miss."

"No," she says sharply. "I've already gotten way too fat." She tries to smile, to shake it off, reaching for her water glass.

"Vi, come on."

Tense blue eyes train on me.

"You are beautiful." Even more so now, if possible, with a healthier lushness instead of that worrisome fragility. But we don't talk about that. "You'd have to gain at least a hundred pounds to be anywhere near fat," I try to joke, covering one of her hands with mine. "And even then, you'd still be beautiful."

She shakes her head again, watching me with a slight frown. "It's so different, out here with you. Like a little bubble, where nothing else matters. It's wonderful, but... How long can we do this?"

"As long as you want." I squeeze her fingers for emphasis. "As long as being here, and the beach, and milkshakes make you happy. I love you," I say, and she smiles, her acceptance spreading warmth through me. "If you don't want to see your friends tomorrow, we can do something cheesy and touristy instead, like going to the Empire State Building."

Her exhale is half chuckle, and she pulls her hand from mine to toss a leftover fry at me.

I pick it up and take a bite, holding her gaze. She laughs, and I drop the rest of the fry. That bubble she mentioned, it's us. Just us. And one day in the city can't break that.

CHAPTER EIGHTEEN

GREENFIELD'S EXPRESSION IS CAREFULLY BLANK as he steps inside the patient room, an air of professionalism clinging to him like his white lab coat. But the results are good. They have to be. I haven't missed one treatment in over a month, stepped up my cardio…

"You've gained weight," is the first thing out of his mouth. But the tighter fit of my jeans and even my bra already told me that. "Which is great. Wonderful, in fact. It'll help your body keep fighting." In the face of my silence, he adds, "Adrian has been good for you."

I nod, gripping the edge of the vinyl table beneath me. It's true, in many ways. The weight gain is good for me, technically—part of the goal, even if an expanded waistline is all my friends would see. Will see, later, when I meet Finley and Prue at some new dessert place Prue found.

"That being said," Greenfield continues, and I tune back in. "Your numbers haven't improved. They're holding steady," he adds quickly when my mouth opens to protest, "which is good. We've stopped the downward slide. If you keep on this way, stay consistent with your treatments and your diet, I'm hopeful we will start to see your body recover, and those numbers come up."

He isn't saying anything I haven't heard before, for most of my life, really. It's been a while since I've been this disappointed by the news, though. I've been working so hard, being adherent, taking care of myself every way I—or modern medicine—know how, and all it's led to is the numbers not dropping? It should have been more.

I can bike farther without getting winded, without needing to stop, so why don't the tests show that?

"Violetta." Greenfield interrupts my thoughts, and I blink back the prickling in my eyes. "This is *good* news. It's step one, and you have to keep working, keep following the plan. Something tells me the Hamptons are more fun than the hospital. And the salt air, it could be helping here as well. So for once, I can tell you to keep doing what you've been doing. Okay?"

I nod, not sure what to say. He's right; I've heard worse news how many times before? And all it's done is make me want a shot of Kahlua in my coffee.

But now, with Adrian, I want more than stopping the downward slide. I want more time.

"No." Grayson leans back in his chair, ignoring the blintzes set on the square table between us.

"No?" I echo. It never occurred to me he wouldn't agree. "Look, I know you've been angry with me, but really? I need your help."

"No," he repeats, no humor edging his answer or his expression. This isn't him pulling my leg, or setting me up for some joke only he'll find funny.

This isn't a joke to me either.

"Why?" The word pops out, unleashing a stream of others. "Because I've taken away your source of amusement? Because you don't get to watch me pine anymore?" Is that all I've been to him—paid entertainment? "It's *better* for her there. She's doing better! Even the air is healthier for her..." I trail off, desperation choking me.

Grayson's been kind to me, I know, letting me live rent-free, connecting me with his vast network, helping me get my foot in the door at Lynch & Co. Introducing me to Violetta, unintentionally or not. I owe him more than I can ever repay, and he's never asked me to even try.

But I need this money. It's not even *for* me, and he has it to give. Normally he'd agree without a second thought.

"Look," I say, straining to keep my tone calm, "I will agree to whatever terms you'd like. Please, if our friendship means anything to you..."

"Go back to work," Grayson says, idly sipping his coffee from impractically delicate porcelain.

"I can't." And he knows that. "I can't work in the city and be with her in the Hamptons, it's not possible." Every day with Vi is a gift. After using up my vacation days, I took a leave of absence. Easiest decision ever, and what I do with my life is my call.

Spending every spare moment scouring random remote jobs has helped keep things at bay, but any hint of savings I had will be gone as soon as I pay for another month at our Hampton hideaway. I will find a way to pay back every cent, but I need him to loan me this money.

"Grow up," Grayson snaps, his cup clinking against the saucer. "Maybe you love her, but you're throwing your life away.

All those shiny dreams you've worked for all these years. And despite your bullshit accusations, I'm not going to sit back and let you do it. If Vi cared for you at all, she wouldn't either."

He shakes his head, frowning. "It isn't her fault, this life she's used to, and her normal choice in men can afford it. But now she's sucking you dry. So go back to work." He pauses to toss a couple bills onto the table and stands. "Before I start charging you rent."

"How'd it go?" Adrian asks as soon as I'm inside.

I drop the stack of mail that's piled up onto a side table. "Fine."

Concern draws his eyebrows together, and he sets aside his laptop but doesn't ask me to elaborate.

I move further into the apartment—my apartment, though it feels a little strange, being back—and drop my bag onto the couch. It was fine, all of it. The appointment, technically, even if I expected better news, and listening to Finley and Prue gab about everything that's been going on, plans for Finley's up-coming party. Even the alcohol-infused fruit tarts with their gold leaf finish. All of it went fine, but somehow, even without our now daily bike ride, I'm just worn out.

"Hey." Adrian's soft voice draws me back to the moment, and I blink a few times to refocus on him. "C'mere," he says, smiling despite the fatigue etched into his expression too. He shifts his laptop to the other side as I move closer, a listing on Upwork showing on his screen. I frown, but he tugs me onto the couch, fingers intertwining with mine. "Doing okay?" he asks.

I nod then scrub my free hand over my face, unable to match the easy contentment already filling his eyes.

"Delivery and a movie?" he suggests, gently squeezing our fingers together.

An exhale is all the agreement I can give. Adrian's smile slips. "I'm going to go lie down for a while," I manage to say.

He kisses my hand before letting me go. I grab my phone from my purse and head to my bedroom. The smaller room's door is closed, but I have no doubt all the equipment we packed into the car this morning is there waiting for me.

Just like the hundreds of photos on my feed have been. I've posted a few pictures of the beach, but the nearly indistinguishable shots from the parties I left behind haven't interested me much. Though it does look like the girls had fun Sunday at the spa. And Finley's upcoming exotic animal–themed masquerade sounds promising. But Adrian and I could come back for that. Much more fun than a doctor's visit and tests, that's for sure. And the rest of it isn't worth leaving the Hamptons.

I let the phone drop and scoot lower on the bed, truly lying down. Adrian's tried to hide it, but I know he's been worrying about the money, the costs of staying in our little cottage. Especially since he took an unpaid leave.

Adrian would never ask, of course, but it would be good to take a bit of pressure off his shoulders so we can stay out in the Hamptons a little longer. Selling my apartment for some temporary financial freedom would be too impractical, and the thought of renting it out on one of those homestay vacation sites is just too sketchy for me to handle.

My gaze wanders to the armoire, filled with gifts from my former beaus. Selling some of them could help, even though it's not quite as easy as going to a pawn shop, not if I want to get anything close to their worth. Still, maybe I could put some feelers out before we leave the city, follow up if we do come back for Finley's party, or by email.

There's a small fortune in jewelry tucked away in the velvet-lined drawers—one I'm more than willing to trade for more carefree days with Adrian.

Vi nudges a nearly empty carton of shrimp lo mein away from her and leans back with a satisfied sigh. Her back arches as she stretches her arms up before working her hair tie out then twisting the long locks into a fresh bun. She drops her head on my shoulder and reaches for the remote, like it's the most natural thing in the world for us to be snuggled up together. And nowadays it is.

The New York tension that fizzled between and around us has already been pushed away by the return of our little bubble. Warm, satiated, content... The two of us are worth the nuisances of the real world, the costs. And regardless of Grayson's *no*, I will find a way.

Chapter Nineteen

When Adrian comes in with the groceries, I shut my computer so he won't see the screen. We've both been doing that a lot lately. And we'll both be able to stop soon. The auction in a couple days should bring in enough to keep us afloat while the pieces I put up through an online broker attract buyers.

Adrian drops some mail beside me, and I tilt my chin up for an easy kiss. He lingers, savoring the kiss as if it's been days and not hours since our last one. A soft hum follows his lifting away. I'm not sure whether it's him or me.

"I'm going to jump in the shower," he says, then tilts his head toward the stairs in obvious invitation. The naive, timid, awkward shell has fallen away entirely. He surprised me—far more adept than his innocent blushes would have had me believe—but I shake my head this time. I prefer our bed, anyway.

Adrian whistles on his way up the stairs. My fingers reach for the mail as I chuckle. The top envelope is an invitation to Finley's party. I haven't decided yet if we should go, but it's not like I have to RSVP.

Beneath an advertisement for a local grocer lies a second envelope, this one odd—plain. Hand-addressed to me, and missing a return label. Our circle still sticks with mailed invitations or occasional thank you notes, hand-delivered on behalf of those trying too hard, but who in the world would hand-address a letter nowadays? Almost no one even knows where to find me out here.

A frown etches itself into my face as I open the envelope and pull out several sheets of stationery with a faded vine printed at its edge. A loopy script covers the pages.

Dear Violetta,

We haven't met, but still I pray you'll read this letter to its end. I am Adrian's mother. He spoke about you in the past, a bit. Lately we haven't heard much from him. Because he's been with you.

It isn't hard to find you on the internet, photos and even articles detailing your life, your choices, every move you make. That cannot be easy for you, but it has helped me, I feel, to get to know you, as much as I can from afar. I have seen you on the arms of tycoons, surrounded by your glittering friends. It makes me wonder why. Why would you choose my Adrian?

Maybe you wanted a break, from the whirlwind life chronicled by everyone who sees you. Maybe you see what's special in my son, something worth leaving that sparkling world behind. Perhaps you even love him, for now. In fact, I hope you do.

I hope you love him, so that you can see what I see, understand why I had to write you. Because I love him too. Him, and my daughters.

Ever since leaving home, Adrian has worked tirelessly toward his dream of becoming an architect. He's been distracted occasionally, sure, by the allure of luxury, of a life like yours and Grayson's, but ultimately he never strayed from pursuing his goals, and meeting the obligations those goals required.

Maybe with the life you lead you do not know this, but for many families, like ours, sending a child to school, even one as determined and hard-working as Adrian, is devastatingly expensive. Adrian studied hard and earned his scholarships, but his schooling, life thousands of miles away, its price was still steep. It was worth the hardships, and he has always made us proud. Until he left his job, for you.

Years of work, thrown away like garbage. And the cost of providing for you, your lifestyle, has jeopardized our lives, too.

You do not know us and have no reason to care, maybe, but please, take pity on our family. We have struggled, keeping our home, a roof over the heads of our daughters. Since starting work, Adrian has eased our burden, like a good son. The son we raised him to be. But we can scrape by without that help, we can find a way.

What we cannot do is take on the burden of Adrian's loans—loans we happily cosigned, knowing our son would never be remiss in his payments. Except now, out of work and financing your beach vacation, that isn't possible. If we have to shoulder this burden, we will lose our home.

Please, Violetta, I am begging you, think of our daughters. And if you cannot care for them, then think of Adrian, of the future he is throwing away to entertain you. All those years invested, for nothing if he tosses it all away now.

Adrian believes himself in love. And in his youth and foolishness, he isn't thinking of the future—when your interest fades, or life simply moves on. And so he's happy to throw it all away for your sake. To make you happy.

But please, if you care for him at all, don't ruin his life. Stop him from sucking every resource dry. Take pity, on his inexperience, his potential, and his family.

Take a moment to consider the consequences he cannot see, is unwilling to consider, and then please, give my son back the life he's worked for. Set him free.

Maura Thompson

A door shuts upstairs. The sheets have fallen from my hand, one by one, covering the table and my laptop as I read. Blindly I tuck the pages back into their envelope, their rustling hiding the sounds of Adrian's movements.

Gasping air, unable to face his cheerfulness, I find my way to the downstairs bathroom and lock myself inside. The cool tiles soak in the overwhelming heat of my skin, sticking lightly.

What am I supposed to do, with pleas like this? Money is a concern, yes, and I am handling it, but the life of his family?

I didn't even know Adrian had sisters. I'm not sure I've ever mentioned mine.

He chose to do this, to come out here with me, and why shouldn't I leave it at that? Our happiness, it has to be worth something, worth fighting for. He was right about that.

And yet…

I didn't know the cost was this—his future, his life, his family. Everything he's ever wanted.

Everything I can never give him.

What kind of life will he be left with when I'm gone?

No temptation of empty luxury could pull me away now from the joy of being held in his arms, of every touch, and smile, and instant of unwavering devotion… Of being loved.

But when I die? What will he have then?

He would do anything for me. But can I let him?

His mother may not believe it, my friends may not understand, but the truth is, I would do anything for him, too.

He'll never return to New York while I'm out here, and he'll fight me if I say I want to leave the salt air, the calmer life, our bike rides to the beach. It *has* been good for me.

And it's destroying him.

These months of happiness we might be able to buy aren't worth the destruction of the rest of his life.

Before I can talk myself out of it, I pull my phone out and type a quick message to William, stuffing my free hand into my mouth to cover the sobs Adrian can never hear.

`I'm sorry. I miss you.`

CHAPTER TWENTY

THE SCRAP OF PAPER SLIPS from my fingers, striking the table as I choke back air.

I made a mistake. This life isn't for me. Don't call.

The scribbled words squirm their way between my ribs, slicing at my heart. Numb, my fingers reach for my phone, calling her automatically, but of course she doesn't answer.

Why didn't I see this coming?

Vi went to bed early last night, sure, but she gets tired. And I didn't hear her get up, or that telltale hum of her treatment. I didn't think anything of it until I saw the note resting on my computer.

Not even then. Stupidly, I thought she just ran out for Danishes or something.

I grab the terse goodbye and plod upstairs to the nook we set aside for her treatments. Bright, airy, with birds popping by to the feeder outside… Cheery, not locked away like in New York.

But none of it is there now, the plush window seat empty and alone.

Why would she want to go back? We've been happy here; I know it.

This life isn't for me.

Was she bored? The bike rides, and days by the beach, and a quiet life with me… It wasn't the excitement she's used to, but we could have gone back to New York any time. Wasn't there an invitation in yesterday's mail? A night here and there spent in the city would have been doable. Unless she didn't want to be seen with me.

The paper crumples in my hand as I call Grayson. By the third ring, I know he won't answer. Between our fight and his loyalty to Vi, Grayson won't be on my side in this. He got bored with the story as soon as it stopped being a hopeless chase.

She's sucking you dry, he claimed.

But without her, there's nothing left.

I couldn't have been nothing more to her than a temporary distraction. What we had was real.

But maybe it wasn't enough.

Some small, bitter part of me points out it's good this happened before next month's rent was due.

Was that the point?

I made a mistake, she wrote, the words both devastating and maddeningly vague.

Is money the only thing standing in our way?

CHAPTER TWENTY-ONE

SOMETHING INSIDE ME WITHERS as I approach William's table and shoot him a smile. He stands, lips brushing the air beside each of my cheeks before we lower to our chairs. It's cold, dispassionate, but then there never was anything more between us. The mechanics work, and we look great together. As if to prove my point, a paparazzo's flash blinks from just beyond the hostess's station.

A waiter places a pot of silver needle tea beside me. William already has a glass of whiskey. It's nearly effortless, slipping back into these roles. Barely a hardship, rejoining the world of luxury I'd left behind. Nothing to complain about. I've missed the theater, too.

Not as much as I'll miss him.

I shake the thought away, sipping my tea. This is the real world; this is what matters. "How have you been?" I ask.

"I don't have much time, Violetta. I agreed to meet you. Why are we here?"

Words clog my throat, and I reach for the napkin as my shoulders shudder with the ripping cough. Hours back in New York, and already…

William adjusts his cuffs as he waits for my answer.

When I can breathe again, I tilt my head and offer up another smile. It isn't about passion or love, but it is about pride—his. "I told you last night. I miss you." The lie feels like choking on slime. "You've been so busy lately. Things felt too settled, I guess, so solid and"—I shrug innocently—"predictable. I wanted some time away from the city, something new."

And it was, with Adrian—exhilarating and heady. Incomparable. But it has to be over.

"I was wrong," I tack on for good measure. "Nothing's as exciting as my life with you."

The waiter arrives with impeccable timing, drawing William's gaze away before he can decide I'm lying. After ordering, he says, "You look well."

I duck my chin rather than respond. Once the paparazzo's photos make it online, speculation will follow about my weight gain, no matter how much Greenfield insists it's good for me.

"It won't be like it was," William says.

The moment freezes—have I well and truly burned this bridge?—but then I manage to raise my eyebrows curiously.

William reaches into his suit jacket and produces a small velvet box. He doesn't open it. "I'll take you back," he says, "but only as my wife."

An inhale is all the answer I can muster. *Marry* him? After finally knowing love…

William's expression is implacable.

"We don't even know," I point out haltingly, "if I'll be… here, if we planned a wedding. Planning so far ahead, it's not possible for me. You know that." Tears prick my eyes, for the future I could have built otherwise, with Adrian.

But William must take them as tears for him, for us. He flips the box open and turns it toward me. Inside, a large marquise diamond framed by rubies and set in platinum gleams coldly.

"No one can plan an event like you, Vi. We can do it soon." He closes the box and moves it closer to me. "The next event you hold at my side will be our wedding, or none at all." He stands, bending down to brush my cheek once more. "Think about it," he adds, then strides out of the restaurant.

The waiter hovers at my side a moment later, staring bemusedly at William's empty chair.

"I'm so sorry, he was called away. Please, pack it all up." I can't imagine taking the dishes home, choking down the reminder of his businesslike proposal, but the pair panhandling down the street would no doubt appreciate the fresh meal. "You have Mr. Braxton's card information. And please have someone call me a car."

"Of course," the waiter murmurs, backing away with the plates he never even set down.

I tuck the velvet box into my purse without looking at the ring and minutes later manage a smile for the hostess who hands me a paper bag as I pass her station. A black car waits outside.

For all his threats, Grayson hasn't touched the apartment in Brooklyn. There were a few more days paid up in the Hamptons rental, but I couldn't stomach the thought of haunting those rooms with Vi gone. Expecting to see her reading on the couch or traipsing down the stairs, ready for our ride down to the beach. Sleeping in the bed we'd shared, remembering each moment of our passion—playful, heartfelt, eager, genuine, and every intoxicating combination in between.

Ghosts of everything we had saturate those rooms.

This place with its dull walls and brown furnishings suited me before, and without her, it will again.

But I won't have to suffer this dreary existence long. I have a plan.

Curled on my couch, I stare at the ring—and the stack of bills beside it. Everything William handled, and other men before him, has been forwarded to me. I probably wouldn't have even seen these had I not come back. They wouldn't have crossed my mind. Not the medical bills, or the insurance payment.

The refills for my meds haven't arrived yet either. Probably because William stopped payment. I'll have to call them, all of them. The numbers are astronomical, especially without dipping into the discretionary account William kept for me. I haven't touched it since leaving, of course, but now, it's almost tempting to see whether he's shut it down.

He can't have planned this. The doorman said the pack of bills arrived two days after Adrian and I were last here. Completely coincidental, but it drives the point home: I can't afford to live without pockets like William's. Or his "offer."

I know why he wants to marry me—it would be seen as the ultimate coup, especially after I left him for a "nobody." The most important nobody I've ever met.

No man has ever gotten any promises from me. They all knew I'd move on if someone more alluring came along. William wants to prove he's the best catch there is. I'm nothing more than an asset he wants to acquire rather than lease. He wants to show the world I'm *his*.

For the first time in years, I feel cheap.

Not that there's anything cheap about that ring, or life at William's side. The idea of slipping it on, of accepting his entirely unromantic proposal, makes me want to gag and throw all the windows open at once.

I reach forward and snap the box closed. It's silly, but immediately it's easier to breathe.

He isn't my only option. The pieces I have up for sale should cover these bills, and I can sell more, just like I'd planned. Live off the past while I figure out my future, find my next benefactor. Maybe someone who travels often so I can hang out with friends in his absence, take some time for my heart to heal.

The sense of selling myself for financial security tangles in my stomach. But better I mortgage my short future than Adrian's whole life.

CHAPTER TWENTY-TWO

"VI!" GRAYSON STRAIGHTENS from his couch, ignoring the girl his movement dislodges. She sits up and pulls together the open edges of her borrowed button-down shirt.

"Sorry to interrupt." I try to infuse a bite of humor into the words, but the attempt falls flat.

"Don't be silly." He waves the girl away and comes toward me, still shirtless himself. "Didn't expect to see you here. Get tired of the Hamptons?"

There's weight behind the question. What *am* I doing here? My eyes prickle again. Maybe it's the air of the city, irritating them.

"Get out," Grayson throws over his shoulder to the girl, then wraps one arm around me and leads me to the adjoining library.

He pours me a splash of calvados, but I shake my head.

"What happened?" he asks, uncharacteristically serious. All the years we've known each other, I've almost never seen him without a smirk or a smile. Not even on his visits to the hospital.

My head keeps shaking as I glance around the burgundy and dark-green highlights in this room. He has a good decorator.

"Vi." His hands land lightly on my shoulders, and my eyes find his face. "What's going on?"

"I left him," I whisper, and wetness trickles along my nose. "It was for the best."

Grayson leans away, then knocks back the calvados. "You did the right thing," he says with enviable certainty. "But why now?"

It doesn't take long for me to tell him everything, from William's proposal, to Mrs. Thompson's letter, to my own realization that Adrian's and my bubble couldn't last. I live in the present, but the rest of the world? It has a future to plan for.

Adrian deserves his future.

Grayson's eyebrows lower and draw together. Brackets form around his mouth. "You did the right thing," he repeats. "Adrian's not like us. He's actually put effort into building his life. And he would have thrown it all away for you."

It helps a little, hearing someone else confirm my choice, my fears. Even if I wish he'd tell me to go back, that I deserve the happiness of love. "You can't tell him," I exhale, then sniff.

Grayson reaches for a discreetly placed tissue, nodding.

"If he knows how I feel, he'll ruin it all. Who knows how much time we'd even have..." With one more sniff, I straighten my shoulders and brush back my tears. I meet Grayson's gaze so he can see how serious I am. "Promise me you'll never tell him. That you'll keep him away from me. It's for the best."

Grayson's sharp sigh bounces off the wood paneling around us. "I promise. I won't tell him anything."

✧ ✧ ✧

It's been days. Every morning I wake up hoping my memory is wrong. But she's not there. Sometimes, I find myself wondering if she ever really was, or if I've lost it entirely.

When I told Grayson, all he said was, "It's for the best." He wants me to go back to how things were—not even that, since he hasn't invited me out to any of those lavish events, or even agreed to a simple lunch.

"Are you back at work?" was the first thing he asked the last time I reached out.

"Tell me she's okay," I begged into the phone. She hasn't posted anything or been spotted anywhere I could find mentioned online. I even thought of calling Greenfield, but he's too ethical. It would be unfair of me to ask. And useless.

"She's fine," Grayson claimed. "She's moved on. So should you."

But how can I? Over and over, I try to recall our final moments together, but they're hazy. You never know the last time will be the last. Our final kiss. Her final smile. I can't bear the thought of never seeing her again.

I finger the stack of bills on the small table beside my chair, my one hope to rebuild our happy bubble. This has to work.

CHAPTER TWENTY-THREE

MY SKIN IS GLOWING from today's pampering, but already my freshly massaged muscles are growing tense as the stylist teases and tugs strands of hair into place for Finley's party. It'll be the first time anyone but Grayson—or William, I guess—will see me since my return. I've needed the time to gather myself for the ultimate performance.

Carefree, enchanting, unattainably alluring. That's what I'm expected to be. Especially now that I sent William's ring back. The mirror catches my grimace at the memory of his calculated proposal, and I school my expression.

I pick up my phone and navigate to Adrian's Instagram profile. Grayson helped me Adrian-proof my life—everything from warning the doormen at my building to blocking him from following my social accounts—but I can't resist. Adrian rarely posts, of course. There isn't anything new since some shots we took at the beach weeks ago, but still I need the tenuous connection, to know he's out there, living the life he deserves.

The turnaround isn't lost on me. Once upon a time he'd done the same thing, following my life in snapshots from afar. There were lots more photos on my profile, though, to feed his curiosity, unlike the old crumbs I'm stuck with.

This is the piece of him I get to keep, now. The beautiful cityscapes and bizarre shots of little architectural quirks. He used to light up as he spoke about bits of the city most of us don't even notice, too absorbed in our lives to care.

I stop willing new photos to appear and focus instead on the finishing touches being added to my hair. Adrian asked about tonight's party, but Grayson's held true to his promise. And without the details, Adrian won't be able to crash.

So the only thing I have to worry about is digging up a smile.

Grayson helps Vi out of the town car, and my breathing quickens as my jaw clenches. How could he?

You're not invited, he wrote when I asked about tonight's party. Was this why?

I force the thought away as I cross the street toward them. Finley wasted no time posting a selfie from in front of the Bryant Park Hotel and its unmistakable black-and-gold façade. I'm not dressed according to what looks like their animal theme, but I'm not here to fit in. All I need is to talk to Violetta.

She gasps when I step in her path. Stunning as always, in a bright blue-and-purple dress with peacock-feather details over her breasts and around the hem. More feathers weave through her hair. Her makeup matches the theme as well, coloring her face in a mask of purples, blues, greens, and gold.

Grayson steps forward, blocking me from her—or her from me. "You're not welcome here." He's lowered his mask, but I caught a glimpse of whiskers. With his black suit, shirt, and tie, I'm guessing panther. For once, the menace is there to match.

"I just need to talk to you," I say to Violetta over his shoulder.

Her chin notches up. "There's nothing to say." She edges toward the door, but I step in the way.

"I know you're worried about the money, paying for everything, but you don't have to be, now. Look." I unzip the pouch I've been clutching and flash the thick stack of bills inside. Beginner's luck, fate, or maybe just desperation was on my side in Atlantic City. "It's more than enough, Vi. Months together, right here." And meanwhile I'll get more.

Her lips have parted, her eyes wide at the money. Grayson glances between us silently.

"Please, just talk to me." I let the pouch drift down. "I love you. Whatever you need, whatever you've been missing, I can provide."

Her shoulders straighten, and her expression resettles into an unfamiliar, cold mask. "You could never give me what I want, or need. There's no point in trying. Goodbye, Adrian," she says and walks toward the door as if I never meant anything at all. The doorman holds the glass open, and she strides through without a backward glance.

A tugging at my fingers brings my attention back to Grayson. He's pulled a handful of hundred-dollar bills from my bank pouch. "Security deposit." Pocket change, for him. "Rent's due on the first," he adds before walking away. He murmurs something to the doorman, who looks at me then nods.

I stuff the pouch into the inside pocket of my jacket and turn away, eyes blind to the colorless street. Steel fills my heart.

Love is a fairytale, Violetta told me once. *Live it if you like, but do it with someone else.*

There isn't anyone else, and anyway she was right. Fairy-tales don't last under the crushing weight of reality.

Vi's gone. Grayson with her, and with him my apartment. But they've brought me down from the clouds. I guess I should be grateful for this swift kick out of the callous clutches of the superficial elite.

PART III

CHAPTER TWENTY-FOUR

TO PUT IT SIMPLY, I've changed.

No, Adrian changed me, tearing my heart open to everything I'd told myself I couldn't want—not with a looming expiration date.

Determined to drive thoughts of him from my mind, I threw myself back into the carefree life I'd carefully sculpted, but the idyllic hedonism has quickly crumbled at the edges. Pressure to prioritize my friends' merriment over the demands of my body chafes like it never has before.

I've tried shattering the mystery, finally explaining all my absences, letting them into my world, but it's as if they can't be bothered to remember. Before, they were ignorant by my choice; now, they're ignorant by theirs.

So I fill my time with the champagne brunches and decadent nights bursting with gastronomic delights that taste like sand even as I choke them down. Despite the fallout with William, my admirers are eager to have me back, plying me with alcohol and jewels and promises of weekends in Santorini or Tuscany, all in a calculated display for my newly unclaimed hand. I should be glad my time away hasn't destroyed all those years of hard work. I've stayed the ultimate prize of the elite, and my hesitation in choosing a new suitor has only encouraged the competition.

But after Adrian, I can't bring myself to trade practiced smiles and emotionless sex even for financial security. Not yet.

The jewelry I sold bought me time, like it was always meant to. I never thought I'd spend that time alone.

Well, almost alone. Grayson hovers nearby, his solemn scrutiny a stark contrast to the cheerful playboy he's known to be. But maybe all of us are faking, playing into the roles we chose.

"We don't have to go," he says, watching from the doorway as I put on lipstick, piecing together the immaculate façade that once was second nature.

"How would that look?" We've attended so many events together, whispers have started. I've postponed confirming the rumors, but it has to be today.

Grayson crosses my bedroom, and soon his hands land on my bare shoulders. "Like we have better things to do."

I wait for the easy smile I still associate with him to flash across his features. But of course, it doesn't. It hasn't in a while, not in private, anyway. "I'm sorry you have to—"

He cuts me off, "It's not me I'm worried about."

He means me, but my mind jumps to Adrian. Will he hear of our lie and think it's true? Does he already? All I know is he's moved out of the apartment Grayson let him use, and they haven't spoken since.

My head shakes as I clear the memory of his bewildered heartbreak, then I paste on a smile and meet Grayson's gaze in the mirror. "If you haven't changed your mind, then tonight is our last chance."

It didn't take long for William to find a replacement. Of course Karolina was more than willing to oblige. But at least Finley warned me that the Epione Gala in three days will also be the official announcement of their engagement. If I have any hope of remaining Violetta Dorée, with all that name has come to mean, I can no longer appear unattached.

Grayson squeezes my shoulders and steps away.

I pull myself together and stand, but the pressure-pain in my chest doesn't ease. Holding my breath, I reach for a tissue and signal to Grayson that I need a moment. Before I'm ready, the cough bends me over the vanity, the tissue reaching my mouth mid-motion.

When the outburst eases, I bow my head, eyes still closed, waiting for my heartbeat to settle.

"Vi…"

I manage to glance at Grayson, but his eyes are trained on my hand—and the tissue dotted with red.

"I know, this isn't what you wanted to hear," Greenfield says, eyes filled with an attempt at concerned sympathy that makes me want to scream and tear off his mask.

"It's been days," I protest, as if it's up to him. Almost a week, now, back in the sterile bubble of the hospital. "Even before, I've been—" I can't bring myself to say *adherent* or *compliant* or however else they want to dress up the word *obedient*.

All those hours wasted on my treatments, and for what? My heart pounds in my chest and head, air wheezing out of my lungs and past the plastic tubing attached to my face. "What about another antibiotic?"

For a moment Greenfield's brow furrows, but that blank medical expression soon overtakes what I can see of his face. "As I mentioned, we will be switching your medication again, in hopes we can get the infection under control. That's our immediate goal." He sighs, his gloved hand dropping lightly onto mine, the latex all too familiar against my skin. "It's time to start discussing transplantation, Violetta. Even if—when we beat back this infection, the damage to your lungs... We need to consider all our options, and there's a lot of screening to get through."

My options.

Greenfield must have noticed something in my expression, because he shifts gears, patting my hand. "I do have some good news." He tries to force a smile, cheeks tensing behind the mask. "You have a visitor."

The labored squeak that is my breathing speeds up. He came before...

"I wanted to give you an update before letting him in," Greenfield adds, "but Grayson is here. I'll go get him now, all right?"

A new fissure cracks my heart, but I force myself to nod. Of course Adrian wouldn't have come. He wouldn't even know I'm here. And it's better this way, for him.

A petty triumph, but at least I know: I did the right thing.

CHAPTER TWENTY-FIVE

JAXON LYNCH DRONES ON, and I shake myself out of my wandering thoughts in an attempt to focus. This design might finally give me a chance to show the firm what I can do. A low-profile project, sure, but that's why the senior architects are letting a few of us lower on the totem pole submit designs. The best one will be presented to the clients. I should be focusing, but my thoughts are tangled elsewhere.

Grayson texted me yesterday. A simple "Lunch tomorrow?" but more than I've heard from him in months. I didn't respond, but that hasn't stopped me from wondering why he got in touch. Why now? And why lunch.

Anything Grayson wanted to say after all this time, he could have sent via text. Or email. Or carrier pigeon, for all I care. My fist pummels my thigh under the conference table. I want nothing more to do with him or anything else related to the world of ultra-wealthy, overindulgent, self-proclaimed hedonists.

When the meeting wraps up, I escape quickly out the doors. My design isn't quite where I want it, but I haven't been able to put my finger on the problem. That's all I should be thinking about. With nothing else in my life, there's no reason not to spend another late night at the office.

Back at my desk, I gulp the remaining lukewarm coffee in my mug, then head to the break room for a refill. A once commonplace sight stops me in my tracks. Grayson leans against our office manager's desk, no doubt throwing her the smile that's wrapped countless women around his little finger.

But when he sees me, Grayson isn't smiling.

"What are you doing here?" I ask.

"You don't want to have this conversation here," he says quietly.

"I'm not having it all," I say, turning away.

"You owe me."

The words stop me mid-step, twisting me back around.

"At least a conversation." There's no sign of his customary nonchalance. "Come on. I'll buy you lunch."

For the first time since the day we met, I have an urge to punch him. But already we've drawn the curious eyes of my coworkers. It isn't his reputation my fists would ruin. "Fine," I say and lead the way out of the office.

We don't speak to each other again until we're seated at a nearby deli, my previously forgotten empty mug now on the table between us.

"What do you want?" I finally ask, holding his gaze.

He leans back in his chair, then exhales sharply. "I thought I was helping you, you know. You were throwing your life away, out in the Hamptons."

Bile rises in my throat at his imperious meddling. I may owe him, but... "I'm not your puppet, to be tugged about at your every whim."

Surprise rocks him slightly back, foreign wrinkles appearing on his forehead.

"I appreciate everything you did for me, all the ways you helped me, I do," I grind out. "But my life isn't yours." All the free rent and lavish parties in the world don't mean I could be bought. I'll find a way to pay him back, every cent if he can count them.

He doesn't respond, and the anger of the last months swirls in my gut until I look away to measure my breathing. A young girl sets our orders on the table, but I push my sandwich away. Grayson doesn't reach for his plate either.

"I know about you and Violetta," I tell him, my voice surprisingly steady even though it's the first time in ages that I've said her name. "So if that's why you came…"

A thought hits me, and I can't prevent the bitterness from spilling out. "Or has she tossed you aside too? Did you come to commiserate? Because—"

"I never learned, I guess," he interrupts, "to connect to people without money involved." His head shakes, as if his world has shifted.

Before all this, I would have asked what that means, what he's realized. Personal growth doesn't exactly come easily for him. But I stay quiet.

"That doesn't matter, now," he says. "I never thought of you as a puppet. But when Vi asked… It was for the best, I thought, for you and for her." He laces his fingers together and leans forward, arms braced on the table. "But we were never together."

I open my mouth to contradict him, but he keeps going before I can. "It was an act, to help her return to our little world without marrying Braxton, or finding someone else. Which she couldn't bring herself to do."

Blood rushes to my head, my breathing quickens, and now it's my world that's tilted. But it shouldn't matter; she still left me.

"She made me promise not to tell you." Grayson shakes his head and leans away. "She'd kill me if she knew I was here, but now that she's…"

I can't make sense of the fragments of his thoughts, but my traitor of a heart squeezes painfully. "She's in the hospital again?"

"She was," Grayson says, and the world stops, senseless noise filling my ears until my mind catches up to the fact that his lips are still moving. "…at home. Wasting away as she pines, and all because she cared enough to let you go."

Gripping the edge of the table, I force air through my lungs. Grayson waves away the busboy's concern and nudges my plastic cup of water closer.

If she did care for me… All it's been is wasted time. "Why?" It comes out as a whisper.

Solemnity—or is it the compassion that has been missing these last months?—fills his expression. "A letter. From your mother," he says as if that explains something. "It made Vi realize she was being selfish, not thinking about your future. She wanted better for you than piles of debt. A lost career." He clears his throat, then reaches for his own water, waiting beside his cooling food. "She still thinks it was for the best. I agreed with her at first, but now… It's not looking good," he adds as if I needed the clarification.

"I have to go see her." I'm standing before I realize I moved.

"She's not there," Grayson calls after me, and I spin around. "You just said she was at home."

He nods, standing too. "Home, with her family. Not in Manhattan." He tosses a bill on the table even though we've already paid, unthinkingly generous with his wealth as always. Almost always.

"Where," I force out hoarsely.

"I have a car waiting." He leads the way to a sleek town car, but then he always knew how our conversation would end. What else can I do but go to her? I should have been there this whole time.

Grayson stares out the window as a chauffeur takes us to Violetta, plodding through the streets. He made the wrong choice, keeping me away, but maybe not out of boredom or indifference. Maybe his reasons weren't as selfish as I thought.

As the car heads out of the city, finding a smoother rhythm, he turns and catches me watching him. I should have given him more credit. He should have done the same for me.

But if he did it all for her?

The roiling resentment that punctuated every day since I last saw her seems to dissipate as the car hits a steady speed. Grayson nods once, and we both settle deeper into our seats. Even unsure of our destination, I count the seconds until I see Violetta again, knowing, finally, that they are finite.

CHAPTER TWENTY-SIX

DYING IS BEST DONE AT HOME, surrounded by those who'll notice when you're gone. It's petty and selfish, but I want at least someone's heart to break a little when it happens. And I know it will be soon.

Everyone still hopes that a lung transplant will happen, the miracle to prolong my life. After hours at Columbia staring at the neutral faces of the transplant team, I know better. I'm far from an ideal candidate.

Grayson met me outside after the last evaluation, his face grim as he ushered me gently into a waiting car. As we drove to his place, he threw his arm around me, gathering me close in a casual way that's become entirely habitual. As if by holding on to me he can ensure I'll never slip away. Worry has changed him, too.

"I want to go home," I confessed as the noises of New York's streets permeated the car.

"We can turn around," he offered, instantly leaning forward to redirect the driver.

"No," I interrupted before he could. "I want to go *home*."

It took him a moment, but then he nodded, settling back into the seat as he understood. He helped me pack a bag, and the next day we drove out here, to the house that's barely changed, and the family who never asked to be burdened by my illness.

I moved away to spare them, from the never-ending expenses and paralyzing helplessness. From the shackles of my condition. They deserved better.

They still do.

But in the end, I wasn't strong enough to avoid the comforts of home.

"You're here," Vi says when we come to her open bedroom, filled with pink patterns and stuffed animals, and all those simply charming, girly things no one would associate with the unattainable tastemaker Violetta Dorée. "You always come"—a slow, labored breath—"when I sleep."

An exhausted smile tugs at the corners of her mouth as her eyes shut and she inhales with the help of the plastic tubing looped over her ears, under her nose.

Shock and pain clog my throat. Pressure on my shoulder snaps me out of it, and Grayson squeezes before backing away down the hall. "I'm here," I start to say, but Vi asks, "Am I asleep?" The question knocks my words back down.

"You only come when I'm dreaming," she murmurs, eyes still closed, cuddled in a knit pink-and-purple blanket. Delicate and pale, aside from spots of crimson on her cheeks. "The Hamptons. And London, Florence… All those places we never got to see together. But never here."

"Vi," I croak out in her pause.

Her eyes open, finding me in her doorway, but they're strangely blank, glazed. "It's time, isn't it?" A small sigh. "Time for you to meet…the real me."

Her eyes drift shut again, torso shifting under the blanket as her breathing underscores our silence.

"Take me somewhere else, Adrian. This dream's too sad." Her tongue passes over her bottom lip, tracing the edge a few times before disappearing.

How could things have gotten this bad so quickly? Tears sting my eyes as I cross to her side, settling on the bed to scoop her up. She's oddly light in my arms and heavy on my chest. I swallow past the grief, the bitterness over lost time, the desperate need to hold her tight and never let go.

"You feel so real." Her voice is breathy, as if she'll be asleep at any moment. Will she wake up?

"I am real. I'm here." I press my lips to her hair, straining to keep my embrace loose, comfortable. "I won't leave you again."

"Adrian?" She struggles in my hold, twisting to leverage herself up using my torso. Her hand presses into my chest, as if she thinks I'll disappear.

"I'm here," I repeat.

Recognition floats up from the depths of her eyes. "How?" she exhales. Her breathing quickens with the confusion.

"Grayson." He waited so long. Are these barely coherent moments all we'll get?

What if it had been too late?

"You came?" She pants lightly, lungs straining. "After everything…"

"Of course I came. I love you, Vi." Even through the blanket, her back feels frail under the circles my palm makes. "Everything's okay," I add, though I'm not sure anything will be again. Gently, I press her to lie back down. I don't know how to help, but I know her breathing needs to slow.

"You're really here," she says, relaxing into my arms, her pants gradually getting more even.

"I'm really here. And I'm not going anywhere." I kiss her temple with a quiet *shush*. "I love you, and I'm here," I repeat, over and over until her tension ebbs away so she can rest.

My mouth's dry, and I can tell it's gotten dark without opening my eyes. They snap open anyway. Of course, he isn't there. I knew better, but still pain pulses in my chest. It may have only been a moment, but I believed he came. The dreams are getting too real.

Arms shaking, I push myself up to reach the bedside lamp. It clicks on, lighting the childhood bedroom that feels more like a prison with each passing day.

Beyond the door, the low hum of the TV in the living room blends with the rush of water in the kitchen sink. I take a few breaths, steeling myself to get up.

"Vi?" Grayson fills my doorway.

When he first brought me here, I thought he'd stay for an hour tops then say goodbye. He's been back often, getting to know my family. Daily, I'd say, but the days have blended together a bit. All without a word for the mess I am—a far cry from the girl he's known for years.

"Can I get you anything?" he asks.

"Water. Please."

He walks to the white desk where I used to do my nails more often than homework, then pours me a fresh glass from the waiting pitcher. "You okay?" He sits beside me as I moisten my mouth. He'd understand if I told him about the dream, but I still don't—can't admit how reality is getting blurred.

The water shuts off in the kitchen, but I can't hear anyone talking. "What time is it?"

"Around eight." He takes the glass from me, and my hand drops gratefully to my lap. "Are you hungry?"

"Not really." I should fix my hair, at least run my fingers through it, but the effort doesn't seem worth it. "Have you eaten?" I ask, the lingering impulse to be a good hostess surfacing despite the fact that I can't do anything about it even if he hasn't.

"Vi," another voice says from the door, and my mouth drops open.

My hands overcome their inertia to smooth back the disaster of my hair, even as my eyes prickle. Have I started hallucinating? I turn to Grayson.

He kisses my cheek before getting up and heading out of the room. "I'll leave you two alone." Grayson pauses by the other figure whose name I can't even let myself think but doesn't say anything else before leaving.

Has he really come? And meanwhile I sit here unable to remember the last time I brushed my hair…or my teeth. This morning, hopefully, whenever that was. Too late, I remember the oxygen tube bisecting my face. I hide it with my hands, unable to take my eyes off him. Before I can pull the tube off, his hands cover mine, thumbs brushing the crests of my cheeks.

He sinks down in front of me, keeping my hands in his. "Hi."

"Adrian." The deep-brown eyes of my dreams stare up at me, sadder than I remember. "Earlier… It wasn't a dream."

He shakes his head, swallowing.

Those really were his arms around me, his voice saying the words I've longed to hear for months. "I'm sorry—"

"Shhh," he interrupts, getting up from his crouch to join me on the bed. "There's no need—"

"No," I cut him off, and he falls silent. "I'm sorry I hurt you." I pause, but looking into his face, having him near after so long, I can't bring myself to tell him that I'm not sorry I left, not sorry that he rejoined reality unshackled from me.

He nods, so incredibly serious. "Let's be clear on something. I'm here now, and I'm not going anywhere."

Warmth blooms in my chest, and I'm not strong enough to fight him, to send him away again. I squeeze his hands, and they don't disappear under my touch. I look away from the devotion in his eyes, turning toward the nightstand, but my phone remains silent. One miracle made me wish for another, a perfectly timed lifesaving call, but of course the real world doesn't work like that.

"Are you hungry? You should eat something," Adrian says, standing up.

"No," I whisper, clinging to him. I can't lose him again now that he's here. "Don't leave me," I say louder.

He gathers me against his chest, murmuring, "I won't. Don't worry." For a moment there's nothing but us, rocking together, his hand massaging through my hair.

"Have dinner with me," he invites quietly, as if I'm desirable—or even presentable—company. "There must be a good burger place around here somewhere," he coaxes, pulling back a bit to see my response. "I could get you a milkshake."

The memory makes me smile, but still I have to blink back tears. "How could I resist?"

CHAPTER TWENTY-SEVEN

VI STIRS IN MY ARMS, and I smile. We fell asleep like this, the most natural position in the world. I'm not sure how long I've been awake, but nothing could draw me away from her now.

Grayson left soon after last night's dinner. I'll have to settle things with him, make amends maybe, but that's not what today is for.

Vi's body stiffens with the alertness of a sudden awakening, but seconds later she relaxes into my embrace. Her hand comes to my arm, squeezing with the faintest pressure as if still needing the assurance that I'm here. I need it, too.

"G'morning," I murmur into her hair. Chill November sunlight fills her room, washing away yesterday's oppressive air of illness, bolstering the certainty deep inside my chest that things will turn around now that we're together.

Vi's ribcage expands with her breath, pressing her against me. "That's it? Pretty unimaginative."

I chuckle at the reminder of the first time I called her. It's going to be a good day. "Your mom came in a little bit ago. Offered to make pancakes for breakfast."

"Then I guess we have to get up."

I loosen my hold as she repositions her arms beneath herself, careful not to snag the plastic tubing reaching to the oxygen tank. Gently, I support her torso as she leverages her body into a sitting position.

Our usual ease is there, if buried, her eyes rarely leaving me as we get dressed. But she laughs at the mess my makeshift toothbrush—i.e. my finger—makes of my face, and the missing months fall away.

Worry still lines the faces of her parents, of her younger sister, as we join them in the kitchen. But even they can see the difference in Vi today, and soon warm conversation surrounds the table. When Vi reaches for a second pancake, her mom flashes me a smile filled with relief, or hope, or undeserved gratitude.

Once everyone's eaten, we're shooed out of the kitchen, but instead of holing up in her bedroom, I bring Vi out to the back porch. Her parents provide blankets and pillows to pad the large wooden bench and keep us warm. We settle in for some peaceful time in the crisp air. The undercurrent of natural sounds surrounds us as I read from her tablet.

My hand drops when Vi twists weakly in my arms to glance up at me. "I missed this," she says with a small smile, her head dropping back to my chest.

"Me too." The simple truth of how desperately I'd needed her back in my life sinks into me, and I don't resume reading.

Anger, bitterness, resentment—every emotion that kept me from plummeting into the hole that her dismissal had torn through my core now crumbles away with seeing her smile, having her near. Feeling her body pressed against the length of mine as our bubble slowly grows, sheltered between us but determined to encompass us once more.

✧ ✧ ✧

Adrian's lips caress mine lightly. I smile as he pulls away, then let my body sink fully into my mattress. "Go," I murmur, but he settles beside me on the bed, lifting my hand in his. It's just a nap, not worth this concerted care, but still I curl my fingers around his warm, steady hand.

"What do you want to do when you wake up?" he asks, not shrinking away from the countless changes that have ravaged my body in our time apart. I could look at his face, into those tender eyes for the rest of my life. I would, if I could keep my own eyes open. But he'll be there, waiting, after I get a bit of rest.

"Take a drive, maybe." A hassle I wouldn't put my parents through, but I know Adrian won't mind. "I could show you around, show you where I grew up. There's a lake, not far." Where I had my first kiss, ages ago. Now I'll take the last man I ever want to kiss there—full circle.

"We could have a picnic in the car," he suggests, squeezing lightly as I nod, my eyelids grown too heavy for me to fight. "You rest," he says quietly. "And when you wake up, we'll take a ride through town, and we'll have a nice afternoon by the lake. Maybe stop for milkshakes on the way back."

It sounds right. Exactly what I want—just Adrian and me, enjoying the sunset, the calm of the lake, and being together. A perfect day.

I take a deep breath, steeling myself as I reenter Vi's home. Her mother helped me pack up a great "picnic" for later. And her father agreed to help me run one more important errand, despite the hesitation in his eyes. Anticipation jitters through me, and I pat my pocket for the millionth time since leaving the jewelry store.

"I'm not sure she's awake yet," Vi's mother says when she sees we're back. Her father greets his wife with a one-armed hug and a soft kiss on the temple. The strain of the last weeks, of years of worry for their daughter, marks their expressions, their posture. But above all of that, I see their love.

"I'll go check," I offer, and they nod as if they've known me for months instead of hours.

There's no answer when I knock on Vi's door, but maybe she's more tired than we expected. Or maybe less time has passed since she lay down than my nerves would have me believe. I crack the door open anyway, and there she is, resting on the bed like when I left. I should leave her in peace, but I step into the room, just to steal a few extra seconds at her side.

She doesn't stir when I brush a strand of hair away from her forehead. Suddenly something about the silence feels off. I shake my head and drop my hand, staring at her face, struggling to piece together the problem right in front of me.

"Oh dear Lord," I hear behind me.

My gasping exhale echoes in the air, and finally I know what's wrong.

People jostle around me, frantic calls for an ambulance mingling with their sobs, and all I can do is stare at the tinge of blue in Vi's face.

Someone pushes me aside, an authoritative voice burrowing into the chaotic stillness of my mind. "She isn't breathing."

Chapter Twenty-Eight

IT HAPPENED QUICKLY AFTER THAT. A master at assembling an event in life, Vi left no detail to chance in death.

The small service was attended by the most exclusive list of guests. With every decision made in advance, Grayson told us all where to show up and when. Only he, Greenfield, Finley, and I joined Vi's family at the graveside. A huddle of black on a gray day, we watched the body that betrayed her lowered into the earth.

With a whisper unbefitting the vibrant zeal of her life, Violetta Dorée—née Violet Dorsey—was gone.

Chapter Twenty-Nine

"SHE LEFT ALMOST EVERYTHING TO YOU," Grayson says, ushering me through the door to his place in Manhattan.

"What are you talking about?" I don't remember how we got here. Did we say goodbye to the Dorseys before leaving?

"Her apartment, the furniture. Most of the jewelry is earmarked for her family, with recommendations on what to sell to cover expenses, though I guess any recent pieces might not have been included. Certain dresses, too, she left to her mom or sister, or for them to sell."

"You think this matters? Right now, you think that's what anyone cares about? What they *get*?" He might as well have been listing the chemical components of brick for all I care.

He frowns, the expression almost comical to my jumbled brain. All wrong for his face. Wrong, like everything else is now.

"What do you want me to say?" he asks.

I shake my head. There's nothing to say, for anyone to say. Nothing that will change anything, or make it better that she's gone. Nothing to bring back the weeks wasted, miles and lifetimes apart.

"It should have been me," I say eventually, unable to bear the silence. "There, with her."

"She didn't want you there," he replies, twisting the shard of misery deeper into my heart. "And then, sometimes, it was the thing she wanted most in the world."

He moves to his sideboard to pour himself a drink. "And each time, she put your future first. She didn't want you trapped in her illness with her."

The crystal decanter clunks against the lacquered surface, a cold, harsh sound. Too harsh, for a room filled with treacherous sunlight. Not harsh enough to break into a world overlaid with an impenetrable ice blue.

"Why you?"

Grayson's small sigh slices through the air. "Because she thought it wouldn't break me, like you or her family. That I wouldn't be torn apart, watching her make plans then waste away." He downs the contents of his glass, then looks inside it, grimaces, and steps away from the sideboard. "She needed someone who cared enough to be there, but not so much they'd drown in grief. And she trusted me to keep you away."

Wood scrapes as he opens his roll-top desk, inexorably continuing on. "You can hate me, but all I did was respect her choice. And I didn't want either of you to go through this alone."

My head bobs awkwardly on my neck. It all makes sense in the way that nothing does when the world has been shattered but the pieces continue to grate against each other, determined to keep functioning. Without her.

Grayson's hand appears in front of my face, holding a scrap of white, blocking my blurred view of his herringbone parquet floor. "She left this for you."

I crane my neck up to look at him, my gritty eyes straining to focus, begging him for something—anything—to make this better in a way my mouth can't. I'm caught between resentment for all the wasted time and gratitude that he was there, helping her. There to get me before it was all too late.

He frowns, then puts the small envelope in my lap, dropping his free hand onto my shoulder. I grit my jaw as my lungs strain to maintain a steady flow of air. Why bother when she'll never breathe again?

My thumb slides over the tiny violet printed on the seal.

"I'll give you a minute," he says, and I watch his footsteps cross to the hallway and disappear.

The paper has creased under the force of my grip. It drops as my fingers let go, unwilling to destroy this lingering part of her.

Whatever she wrote inside, I have to know as much as I can't bear to see it. What do you say to someone as you're dying? Still alive but knowing your words won't reach them until you're gone and buried—what would you write?

The envelope is thin, light. As if she had no energy for the note, or maybe just not enough to say. Did she try to make me hate her once more, one last misguided attempt to "save" me? As if reading whatever's inside could magically make it better that she's gone.

I can't tear my eyes away from the fragile message waiting on the floor. My hand reaches for the envelope, brings it up to my face. Nothing marks it on the outside aside from her floral seal.

Eyes closed, I can still feel the envelope's seams, the tug of the words inside, imbued with endless power until they face the light.

My finger slips under the seal, and the envelope creaks as it pops open, releasing its inhabitant. I breathe through the ache in my chest and pull out the single folded slip of paper.

A shadow crosses the window, reminding me to blink, to move. To open and read the last words I'll ever hear from the woman who brought my heart to life.

Chapter Thirty

Sweet Adrian,

You may think it cruel, reminding you of the hurt I caused you all those weeks ago. I've thought of you constantly. But for your sake, my stubbornness prevails, and this is as close to you as I will let myself get. Knowing you'll see this only after I'm gone lets me be honest when I tell you I want you to move on, to have the life you always deserved.

How long has it been since the last time we were together? Since our last kiss...

Please, don't blame Grayson. I asked him to keep you away, too weak to set you free a second time.

I couldn't bear the thought of dragging you down into financial ruin, destroying your career, your future, when all I would do—all I could ever do—was abandon you. I couldn't selfishly cling to the happiness you brought me, to those extra days or weeks we might have had together, knowing the cost you'd have to bear alone.

I sit now, sometimes, in this home that hasn't changed in the years since I've been gone, and cling to the memories of us. Day after day, I replay each moment in my mind, determined not to let them slip away.

But somehow I can't remember if I ever told you. I hope at least deep down you knew—

I love you, too.

— Acknowledgements —

My deepest gratitude:

To Kris & Rachel, whose names will be all too familiar to readers of my previous books. Are you sick of me thanking you yet?

To the ladies of my writing group, for bravely diving in even before the characters had names.

To Christa at Paper & Sage, for creating the perfect cover without even knowing it.

To the friends who find ways to stand beside me.

To my mom, without whose influence this story wouldn't exist, and to the other members of my family who continue to support me and my writing.

— About Aria —

Aria Glazki's first kiss technically came from a bear cub. Though no fairytale transformation followed, she still believes magic can happen when the right people come together—if they don't get in their own way, that is. So now Aria writes heartfelt romances about relatable people overcoming real-world obstacles to build love that lasts.

Relatable People — Remarkable Love

www.AriaGlazki.com